TOO YOUNG FOR LOVE

"I want to talk to you, Killy," Tom said. "Something happened the other night that I don't understand."

Killy cut him off. "I know you didn't know how old I was when you asked me out. You don't have to let me down easy. I understand how you feel."

"Killy, stop finishing sentences for me." Tom's voice was tense. "Will you meet me after school?"

"Listen, I've got to run. And after school I have to get to the library downtown and do some research. I'm going to Italy on spring break and there's so much . . ."

He cut her off. "Do you know what? Now you're *really* acting like a baby."

It was all she had to hear. She slammed her locker door, turned, and ran down the hall.

Too Young For Love

Gailanne Maravel

BANTAM BOOKS
TORONTO • NEW YORK • LONDON • SYDNEY

RL 3, IL age 11 and up

TOO YOUNG FOR LOVE
A Bantam Book / December 1982

ISBN 0-553-22681-9

Published simultaneously in the United States and Canada

Bantam Books are published by Bantam Books, Inc. Its trademark,
consisting of the words ''Bantam Books'' and the portrayal of a
rooster, is Registered in U.S. Patent and Trademark Office and in
other countries. Marca Registrada. Bantam Books, Inc., 666 Fifth
Avenue, New York, New York 10103.

PRINTED IN THE UNITED STATES OF AMERICA

O   0 9 8 7 6 5 4 3 2 1

For my parents and Ari and Alexi

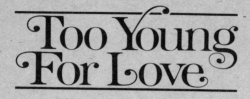

Too Young For Love

Chapter One

The war was over. Killy had won. As she threw the last snowball, her friends Meg and Carrie ran down the sloping driveway to the safety of the road. Then they both laughed, waved good-bye, and started down the road, their heads bent in conversation. *They'll probably be talking about tonight's party all the way home,* Killy thought as she stooped to pick up her plastic bag full of books. She brushed the snow from her parka and walked up the driveway to her house.

When she unlocked the front door, she saw her large gray cat, Timmy Fitzsimmons, waiting for her. "I bet I know what you're waiting for," she said as she turned up the heat in the house, took off her parka, and headed for the kitchen. Timmy was already rubbing his head against the table leg. Then he began pacing up and down in front of Killy and slapped his furry tail against her shins.

"You phony. It's not love you want. It's food."

She fed the cat and put on a pot of water for tea. In a novel she had read last summer, she had been impressed by a scene in which two British girls came running home from school to a table set with tea, warm cakes, and tiny sandwiches. Ever since, Killy had made teatime a tradition. As for what went with the tea, she settled for butter cookies imported from England. They came in a red and white tin with Biscuits written on the front and looked very authentic.

The kitchen was warming up, and Killy could safely remove her soggy outer layer without feeling a chill. She walked to the antique coatrack near the back door and looked into the cloudy old mirror in the center of the rack. Her wavy brown hair was matted from her ski hat. As she tried to fluff it into shape, two strands, as always, vied for position on her forehead.

"You're hopeless, hair!" Timmy lifted his head in response to her voice, licked his white paw, then continued his after-meal ritual. Killy gave up trying to fix her hair without a brush but continued to look into the mirror. *If I had been invited to the party tonight, what would*

I have worn? she wondered. *Maybe the blue cashmere sweater Aunt Jill sent for Christmas. Mom said it was a perfect match for my eyes.*

The sound of water boiling brought her back to reality, and Killy rushed to grab a pot holder. Most of the water had boiled away, but luckily there was still enough for one cup of tea. Twice this year, when she had been deep in thought, Killy had burned pots beyond scouring. Her mother had laughingly decided that a whistling kettle was the only solution, but she kept forgetting to buy one.

Thinking about the party was a waste of good time, Killy decided as she heaped two spoons of sugar into her cup. Kim Lowry's second annual "Think Spring" party! Even the weather had turned out in Kim's favor—or so she said. The last snowstorm of winter, Kim claimed, made everyone look forward to spring. Of course, if it had been warm and raining, Kim would probably have proclaimed she was responsible for the crocuses blooming and pronounced *that* the perfect night for her party.

Not being invited was nothing new to Killy. Two years younger than most of her junior class made her the "baby." Good old Meg and Carrie didn't know she had overheard them asking Kim to invite her at the last minute.

"Are you kidding? That would be like having a baby sister around to report back to Mommy and Daddy. And when it's time to turn the lights down, what would Killy do? Hug her teddy bear?" Kim had laughed and tossed her long, silky, blond hair, which always fell perfectly into place.

Fortunately, not all the kids in her class were like Kim and her crowd. The ones on the school newspaper were fun to work with. When it came down to a tight deadline, it was Killy they turned to for help in smoothing out the rough spots in their stories. And if they were pressed for time because of team practice or a big date, Killy was always willing to take over their assignments. "You can always crank them out, Killy. You're a genius," one of the guys had complimented her one day as he patted her affectionately on the head.

Then there was the football team. At least four of the players called her their academic mascot because she had helped them pass their first-semester English. But none of the boys with whom she was friendly ever asked her out. She was just a little sister to them.

When she did go out, it was to one of Meg or Carrie's occasional parties. Killy was grateful for their friendship, even though in some ways

4

they were an unlikely trio. Meg was reserved, someone who considered every word before she spoke. Carrie was outgoing, with a sense of the dramatic that often bordered on the zany. *I guess I'm somewhere in between,* Killy thought. *That's why we get along so well.*

"Kiddo, I'm home. Killy? Ms. Wyler!" Killy's mother walked into the kitchen and dumped a bag of groceries on the counter.

"I didn't hear you come in. Let me give you a hand."

"You not only didn't hear me come in, you didn't hear me calling you. Daydreaming again, huh?" Her mother smiled at her and managed a quick hug before taking off her raincoat. She wanted to hear about Killy's day.

"My day was like one of those old good news/bad news jokes," Killy said, trying to put the party out of her mind. "Remember the feature story I did that was entered in the tri-state competition? I won first place! Can you believe it? I'll get a certificate, and the school gets one to hang in the newsroom."

"Of course I believe it. I knew that was a good story the first time I read it. And I brought it to work, and everyone liked it. I'm so proud of you." This time her mother stopped unpacking the groceries and gave her a long hug.

"I'll give you a hand. What are we having?" Killy asked.

"Well, if you've finished your tea, we will now prepare to create one of the finest international dishes. Chili!" Her mother affected a British accent that made them both laugh. They started supper.

"You know, Mom, it was good today when I got the news about the award. I was glad I was in the newsroom when the announcement came over the loudspeaker. It only lasted a few minutes, but everyone was congratulating me at once. It was great."

Mrs. Wyler smiled. Then she suddenly remembered something. "You said something about a good news/bad news day. What did you mean?"

"Oh, nothing. I mean, nothing I can't handle. Hey, if you don't mind, I'll go up and do some homework while that's cooking."

"Killy, it's Friday night. You can let your homework go for a while, can't you?"

"No, I really want to get a head start on my chemistry project." Killy started for the door.

"Is there anything you want to talk about? If something happened today, I'd like to hear about it." The kitchen door swung closed, cutting off Killy's sentence about everything being all right.

Upstairs, Killy closed the door to her room. There were days when her comfortable room became a refuge, and today was one of those days. She needed time alone to think about something that had happened right after all the fuss in the newsroom about the award.

Mrs. Gillen, the paper's faculty advisor, had been handing out next week's assignments. "Killy, you're on the Thompson interview. Tom Thompson, the newest basketball star at Ridgefield, remember? I think you're still up in the clouds from hearing about the award."

"Um . . . that's not it. I just wondered, why me? I didn't expect to have to interview a basketball player." Killy was nervous as she tried to explain. She didn't want Mrs. Gillen to think she was too big a "star" now to do routine stories.

Instead, Mrs. Gillen thought Killy was worried because it was a sports story and she might not have enough background to handle it. "Don't worry, you can handle it. We're not looking for a story on how he thinks the team is doing. It should be a story about him—how he feels about moving to a new school and suddenly finding himself the forward who could bring the team into the championships; his interests and his hobbies; and if there are any other athletes in the family. That's the type of thing we want. You'll do fine. Do you know him at all?"

"Not really. I met him once, but I'm sure he doesn't remember." Killy took the assignment sheet.

"Well, you'll get to know him Monday, won't you? Try to set it up for then. There's no practice on Monday."

Mrs. Gillen turned back to read a note she had been handed, and Killy left the room. All at once, it came back to her—why she didn't want to interview Tom Thompson. She was afraid of him. Not afraid of *him* exactly, but of how she had felt the only time she met him.

She and Carrie had gone to a record store. While Carrie had gone off looking for the latest hit single, Killy had been quietly looking through the folk guitar albums. Suddenly a hand reached out for the album she was staring at. Startled, she looked up and saw a curly-haired mountain of a boy. "Hi, I'm Tom Thompson," he said. She just stared and blushed, unable to speak. When she saw Carrie returning, she ran to the cash register to join her. "Nice meeting you," she yelled back to Tom, realizing that she hadn't even introduced herself. She was so embarrassed that she rushed Carrie out of the store. Carrie had asked her about the incident for weeks, but Killy refused to say a word about it.

That weird sensation will probably never hit me again, Killy thought as she sat in her wicker rocker looking up at the ceiling. *I've interviewed kids before. It will be a piece of cake.* But something still worried her. Today, Meg and Carrie had mentioned that Tom was Kim's date for the party. Killy didn't know why she felt angry hearing the two names linked, but that was when she had started the snowball fight.

She got up, grabbed a brush, and began unscrambling her hair. When she finished, she walked to her full-length mirror. Her tall, lean body reflected back at her. The flush in her face from the cold afternoon highlighted her cheekbones. *Who needs parties?* she thought. *Someday it will be Kim who envies me, when I'm a foreign correspondent and sipping tea in London or espresso in Italy.*

But her dreams didn't stop the tear that was running down her cheek. Suddenly she realized that her mother was calling her. The chili was ready.

Chapter Two

His head nearly touched the top of the door frame as he walked into the newsroom. Killy wondered if Tom Thompson had to worry about ducking through doorways everywhere he went.

"Kelly? Am I late? I got your note in my locker this morning about an interview, and I—"

"Killy. The name's Killy, *i* not *e*!"

"What? Oh, your name. I'm sorry, I wasn't thinking. It's written right here on your note. Actually, I didn't see the note until a few minutes ago. I hope I'm not late." Tom put his books down on the table and sat across from Killy.

"It's OK. I mean you're not late, and it's OK about the name. It happens all the time. The '*i* not *e'* just came out from habit. I didn't mean to embarrass you."

Killy was thinking she had never before left a note in someone's locker to set up an interview. Until now she had always asked for interviews in person. Leaving the note for Tom had been a cop-out, a way to avoid meeting him face to face.

"Well, what can I tell you?" Tom's question surprised her.

"About what?" she asked.

"I don't know. You're the experienced one. I've never been interviewed before in my life."

Killy was fumbling but got hold of herself. "Right. Well, tell me how the team's doing." *Dumb,* Killy thought. *It was the one question Mrs. Gillen said didn't need to be asked, and, brilliant me, I've led off with it.*

Tom didn't seem to think it was dumb. He smiled. "Killy, it's looking good. This is the first time I've ever been on a team with even a shot at the championship so I'm happy to be part of it."

Good quote. Things were looking better. "And how do you feel as the forward everyone is counting on to give us a chance for the state title?"

"I didn't realize everyone was counting on

me. I've had some good breaks this season. I just feel lucky there was an opening for me when I moved here. Do you still like folk music?"

"What?" His question threw her.

"Remember the day I saw you in the music store? I'm almost positive you had a folk guitar album in your hand. I remember looking at the cover. It was the one I wanted." Suddenly, *he* was interviewing *her.*

"Yes, I still like it, but I can't believe you remember." Killy was stunned. He had messed up on her name, but he did remember her! He was looking into her eyes, and she was looking right back.

"Ready with your next question?" Tom was smiling at her.

For the first time she noticed how dark his eyes were—or did they just seem dark because his hair was so light in contrast?

"Oh, yes. How did you know you wouldn't hit your head when you came through the doorway?" Killy couldn't believe she had asked this.

Tom fell back in his chair and laughed. "What kind of a question is that? Do you really want to know? Well, I've always figured that door frames are pretty much standard, so unless I shoot up another inch overnight, I'm pretty safe. Had a bad time once on a field trip, though.

We toured one of those eighteenth-century restorations with low-beamed ceilings. By the time I got out of there, I thought my spine was bent for life, and I had this huge bump on my head from running into a stairwell overhang."

Both of them laughed. The rest of the interview followed in the same light spirit. She got what she needed for the story, and as a bonus, she got to know Tom better. He seemed to want to know her better, too. He would answer her questions and then jump in with one of his own. Killy was pretty sure that he wasn't just playing a game with her. He seemed really interested.

"Tell me how you got your name. It's interesting—unusual."

At least he hadn't made a joke! "It was my grandfather's nickname. His last name was Killgore, but everyone called him Killy. My mother liked it so much I think she planned to use it whether she had a boy or a girl."

She began to put her notes away, almost wishing the interview wasn't coming to an end. Tom picked up his books but didn't seem to be in a hurry either.

"Hey, Killy, I'll wait for you while you pack your things up. You have everything?" Tom turned out the light and closed the door as they entered the hallway. They continued to talk quietly in the empty corridor until a loud voice shattered the tranquillity.

"Tom! Oh, Tom, I'm glad I found you. There's something you absolutely *must* hear in the gym. It's a new cheer we worked out using your name!" Kim was bouncing down the hall in her tiny green shorts and white sweatshirt. Her long, golden hair bounced as she moved.

Tom looked hesitantly at Killy. Kim playfully tugged at his arm. Killy shrugged and managed a smile.

"Don't worry about me. I'm headed in the opposite direction anyway. Thanks for the interview." She turned and walked away from them. When she looked back, they were still there. Then she pushed her way through the heavy exit door and let it slam behind her like a clap of thunder.

She took a deep breath and set off for home. There was a slight wind, but unlike last week, this one held some promise of spring. Killy wondered if Kim had already taken credit for the change.

As she walked, Killy was mentally typing out the lead for her story on Tom. He had mentioned working at a stable for two summers before moving to Ridgefield. His work afforded him free riding lessons, and he was beginning to handle jumping despite a few falls. Killy had her lead! *"When he isn't practicing jump shots, forward Tom Thompson is practicing jumping horses."*

The rest of the article would fall into place. If only her other thoughts could be so easily arranged. Had Tom really been planning to walk her home? Why was Kim playing up to him when she already had a boyfriend? *Why am I thinking about this?* Sure the interview had gone well, but he was probably the kind of person who was friendly to everyone.

With only a few more blocks to go, Killy stepped up her pace. It was late for her to be getting home. Her mother would be due soon, and Killy could have teatime set up for them both.

When she saw the lights on, Killy knew her mother must have beaten her home. When she opened the door, she was greeted by the pleasant smell of lemon. And the house was already warm.

"Mom? What are you doing home so early?" She went over and kissed her mother, who was busy slicing bread at the counter.

"I guess it *is* a surprise to find me home and cooking. I got off early. Well, the entire

16

department was let go early. We had a luncheon today and afterward, the boss decided he wouldn't get much more work out of anyone, so he sent us home. I thought it might be fun to bake a cake, fix us some sandwiches, and have a *proper* teatime. See, your imagination is catching. I'd better be careful!"

"Mom, that's great. It's a terrific idea, but this looks more like a meal." Killy eyed the platter of sliced meats, tomatoes, cucumbers, and cheeses.

"That's what I'm counting on. This is really supper, but we can save some for nibbles later if we get hungry." She took the cake pan and turned it upside down on a plate. "And this, I'll have you know, is lemon teacake. I've never made it before, but we had all the ingredients, so I thought I'd give it a try."

"It smells delicious. Maybe we should skip the sandwiches!" Killy headed for the coatrack and jumped when she heard a high-pitched shrill. "A teakettle! You remembered! I promise I won't burn another pot."

They ate and talked, and Killy felt closer to the girls in the English novel than she had ever dreamed. She was really touched that her mother had gone to so much trouble for her.

"I thought you might need some cheering

up tonight." Her mother began to cut a second slice of cake, but Killy stopped her. She was already stuffed.

"I loved all of this, but why did you think I would need cheering up?" Killy was puzzled.

"I met Meg's mother in the supermarket, and she told me all about the big party last Friday at Kim's. I thought today you'd have heard nothing but the rehash of the party and might be down because you hadn't been invited."

"Hey, don't worry about it. It's not the first party I've missed, and it won't be the last. Really, I didn't give it a second thought. You shouldn't either." Killy stood up. "I'll clean up. You have a class tonight at the community college?" She began to gather the dishes and the remains of the teatime feast.

"Yes, I have a class, but I'm not in a rush since we ate so early. And, honey, don't change the subject. I'm sorry you weren't invited. I know it's hard being younger than the other kids in your class, but maybe you could work on making them forget that. I just want to make sure you enjoy your last two years of high school— dating and going to parties and dances. It's a time of life I don't want you to miss."

"Sure, Mom." She took a deep breath to keep from saying what she really wanted to say—to keep from blurting out what it would hurt her mother to hear. How could her mother, of all people, push her daughter into showing an interest in boys? *Look what happened to you,* Killy fumed to herself. *You married your high school steady, got pregnant two years later, and divorced one year after that.* Killy was sloshing the last teacup in the soapy water, over and over again.

"Hey, don't take the design off the cup. You've washed that four times now! Killy, think about what I said. Sometimes you're so deep in your dream world that the kids may think you're unfriendly. All I'm saying, kiddo, is try to be more open." Killy let the water drain out and stood there watching it, hoping her anger would drain with the last of the suds.

Later, upstairs in her bedroom, she could hear her mother getting ready for night class. How many years, she tried to remember, had her mother been going to night school? At least four. On one of the nights she was out, Killy had found her mother's high-school yearbook shoved in the back of a closet. She had memorized the caption under the picture of the pretty, smiling girl who would be her mother: "KATE KILLGORE: National Honor Society; Argosy editor-in-chief; Chorus. Plans a teaching career. Could steady beau Walter change those plans?"

Did he ever! Killy flopped on the window seat and studied the gnarled branches of the apple tree outside her window. Right now, against the dark sky, it looked like an old arthritic hand, but soon there would be pale green leaves and then the blossoms.

Is that what you want for me, Mom? You could have had so much more than a drudge job and years of night school. If that's what dating can lead to, then maybe I'm lucky no one ever asks me out. Maybe.

"Killy?" Her mother poked her head in the door, and Killy could see the collar of her tan raincoat. "That was the phone. Didn't you hear it? It's for you. A boy." She smiled. "I'm on my way out. Don't stay up too late."

Killy tried to walk calmly to the phone in the hall, but her heart was racing.

"Killy? Hi, it's Tom. Sorry about this afternoon. I didn't mean to cut you off like that, but you know Kim. She somehow manages to get her way."

"Yes, I know Kim. It's OK, you didn't cut me off."

"Anyway, Killy, I just wanted to be sure you didn't have more questions."

"No, really. I was finished."

"Oh, OK. Well, I just wanted to make sure. Listen, I really liked talking to you. Maybe we could talk again sometime. I'll see you at school, I guess."

"Sure, I'll see you at school. Thanks for calling. Goodbye."

"Bye, Killy."

Stupid! That's what I am, Killy decided. *Two minutes ago I was convinced I'm better off not dating, and now I feel let down because Tom didn't ask me out for a date! He was just being nice and apologizing, and I started letting my imagination run wild. With Kim of the golden hair chasing him, why would he think seriously about me? Award-winning stupid, that's what I am!*

She slammed her bedroom door behind her and walked to her desk. "Boys! Who needs them?" she said aloud. Then she looked at the plants sitting on the temporary worktable she had set up. They were part of her science project.

"That's what I'm going to do—finish extracting ancient healing substances from plants. It will be the first time anyone has ever done that at Ridgefield!"

Chapter Three

Carrie's red-and-green silk scarf came within a hairline of Killy's macaroni and cheese. They were sitting by an open window in the noisy cafeteria. It was the first day that was warm enough to have windows open throughout the school. Carrie didn't seem to notice how close she had come to ruining her scarf, but Killy did.

"I don't know how you do it, Carrie. A flowing scarf every day and you've never been hung on a doorknob, or tangled in an electric typewriter. Me, I read warning labels and know they were written for me. I could be killed wearing a scarf like that." Killy grinned at her friend, who was anxious to talk to her. Carrie had pursued her through the food line and across the cafeteria, dodging chairs and heads.

"Come on, Killy, be serious. Give me a first line at least. You know I can't write poems." Carrie jabbed at her salad. She had been a vegetarian for two weeks.

"You've got the whole weekend to do it. It isn't due until Monday, right?"

"Killy, you've got to be kidding. What whole weekend? Have you forgotten that tomorrow's the game that could mean the state basketball finals? There are signs in every hall, a banner as big as an elephant across the commons. Where have you been? And Sunday's shot. It's my grandmother's birthday. That means a command performance in Boston, and we won't be back until late."

"Of course I know the game's tomorrow, but I guess I'm not as caught up in it as you are. I work Saturday afternoons, remember? All right, I can see you're not going to let me eat, so tell me the subject of the poem and what kind of verse you're supposed to write."

"Oh, I knew you'd help. OK, it can be anything about spring. It can be free verse or rhyme. Maybe rhyming would be better. What do you think?" Carrie was curling a carrot shaving around her fork.

"Mmm. Did you know rhyming can be a

sign of mental illness?" Killy watched Carrie's expression and started to giggle.

"You won't be serious, will you?" Carrie thought for a moment. "Is it really a sign of mental illness?"

Before Killy could speak, a familiar masculine voice answered Carrie's question. "This is very true—as in true blue. This lady is right about verse. It can be a sign of something even worse."

Tom looked so comical, Killy thought, standing there stroking an imaginary beard and mimicking a German psychiatrist. Even Carrie had to laugh. Tom looked down at Killy. "Hey, I've got to run. Will you be at the game tomorrow?" His name was called, and he didn't wait for her answer. "I'll see you there," he said, then moved along as two kids balancing trays stood waiting to pass.

"I didn't know you knew Tom so well," Carrie said. "How did you meet him?"

"Oh, I don't know him *well*. I met him in that record store. Remember? Then I interviewed him for the paper last week. And you can stop with that goofy look. He was just being friendly, that's all. Let's get back to spring." Killy had no intention of letting Carrie in on what she really thought of Tom—not yet anyway.

25

"Spring? Oh, the poem. Maybe I should go with free verse. I've got it—the party . . . Think Spring. How's this? Think spring, think showers, think birds, think flowers . . ."

"You're rhyming again," Killy said, then burst out laughing. "You're hopeless, Carrie!"

Saturday was dismal. It started with a drizzle that turned into a downpour by noon. The ground was already saturated with the recently melted snow, and the added rain made walking without hip boots next to impossible. Killy was glad her mother had offered to drive her to the hospital.

Tuesday, Thursday, and Saturday afternoons, Killy worked at the hospital bookstore and gift shop. Delivering gift and book orders to the patients was fun. Killy would have done it for free. But she was grateful for the extra money she earned and proud she had landed one of the few paying jobs for teenagers at the hospital. Of course, the fact that her mother knew the manager, Mrs. Clark, had helped.

The rain slowed the crosstown traffic to a crawl. By the time they reached the main entrance to the hospital, Killy was already five minutes late. As she walked quickly through the lobby and past the reception desk, she could see the shop was crowded.

"Sorry I'm late, Mrs. Clark," she said. "I'll hang up my coat and be there in a second." Fortunately, Mrs. Clark was a joy to work for. She was easygoing and never lost her cool, even on the busiest of days.

"Don't rush, Killy. It's bad for the heart. Besides, the patients aren't going anywhere for a while. All the orders are tagged over on the counter."

While she was making her deliveries, a nurse in one of the wards called out to her. "Killy, would you mind doing me a favor? This plant has been here for an hour, and I can't leave the desk. Would you please deliver it to Room 402?"

The plant made Killy and the nurse laugh. It was a scrawny fern with a plastic basketball stuck in the center. Killy hoped whoever was getting it would not be too disappointed.

With her shoulder she pushed open the door to 402. One bed was empty, and when she looked at the other, she almost dropped the plant. It was Tom! He was in traction. He looked pathetic, but all she could do was laugh.

"Please, your sympathy is too much. Why don't you try laughing?" Tom sounded grim, but he was smiling. "What are you doing here, Killy? Wait, that didn't come out right. I just didn't expect you to visit, but thank you for coming."

She walked over to his bed, her eyes still wet from laughing. "I didn't come to visit. I work here. I'm the delivery person! I didn't know you were in here. What happened?" She handed over the plant, and he read the card and laughed.

"Ouch! It hurts to laugh. We were practicing last night, and I collided with someone. I don't know exactly how I did it, but I injured my neck, and they put me in traction."

He was depressed, and she felt terrible for having laughed when she saw him. "Tom, I'm sorry I laughed. And the night before the game . . . today's game! Oh, it's being played right now. You must feel awful."

"Now *you* look depressed. Well, I'm afraid your story will never run. Wasn't it supposed to be a victory story?" Tom studied Killy's face.

"I'll rewrite it. No matter who wins, people still want to know how you feel being a star forward. Now I'll just add what it feels like to miss the big game."

"Hey! Don't you be sad. Aren't you hospital people supposed to bring cheer? You know what

I'm thinking?" Tom started to laugh but winced when it hurt. "Last night, after they brought me in here, the nurse switched on the television. There was this old Bogart movie on—*Casablanca*. Have you seen it? Well, remember that line—'Of all the dumps in the world, she had to walk into mine'? Well, of all the rooms in this place, you had to walk into mine."

"It wasn't 'dumps,' " Killy said, laughing. "That was Bette Davis who talked about 'dumps. No, Bogart said—" Killy couldn't continue because both of them were laughing so hard.

"Well, whatever. It's fun to have you here, Killy. I like it when you laugh. You're so pretty when you laugh."

Killy could feel herself blushing. "Look, you're going to have plenty of visitors later. I know they'll make you feel better. I'd better be getting back. Hey, is this plant worth saving?"

"I think it has a fighting chance. Will you come back?"

"Sure," Killy said. "I don't even have to observe visiting hours. Except for some areas of the hospital, I can come and go as I please, and no one cares. I'll stop by after visiting hours."

Killy closed the door behind her and touched

her cheeks. They were warm. Deep inside her, the same weird sensation she had had the first day she met Tom was returning.

In the four days that followed, Killy was a frequent visitor to Room 402. Tuesday was the only day she had to be at the hospital to work. The other three days she pinned her ID badge on and went to see Tom before or after visiting hours. No one questioned her comings and goings, and she delighted in pretending she was carrying off some great conspiracy.

Tom called her "super sleuth" when she poked her head in the door, checking to see if he was alone. He was always glad to see her and was more cheerful now that the team had reassured him he was not responsible for its 90—60 loss. The game had been a hopeless cause from the start. Tom was convinced that next year would be a different story.

He wasn't as convinced that he would pass chemistry with more than a C, so Killy worked with him on the assignments brought from school. They ate cookies his mother had baked and tackled equations. He was amazed at how quickly she could spot his errors.

"Hey, is there anything you're not good at?

What's your worst subject?" Tom asked on his last night in the hospital.

"Gym," Killy said, and he laughed. "No, it's true. I almost failed field hockey. Quit laughing!"

"I can't. You're funny. How do you almost fail field hockey? You don't look like a klutz."

"That's just it. I *look* athletic. Put me in the goalie position, though, with a herd of girls charging at me with clubs, and I run out of the way. Score one for the other team."

"Sticks, not clubs," Tom managed to say.

"Whatever. They're a potential threat to my body." They were laughing so loud that a nurse came in and told Killy she would have to leave. Now they wanted to laugh even more but didn't dare.

"I've got to get out of here. All I need is for her to report me to Mrs. Clark, and I'm out of a job." Killy stacked Tom's books on the night table and poured the remains of her cup of water on the fern.

Tom reached out and took her hand. He had stopped laughing, but his eyes were smiling at hers. Killy's hand felt as tiny as a child's inside his large, strong one.

"I get to go home tomorrow. The doctor said if I take it easy for the rest of the week, I'll be good as new and back to school on Monday. You've been so terrific to visit me so often." Tom continued to hold her hand.

"Well, I liked coming. It's been fun, and I'm glad you're going home tomorrow." She really *wasn't* glad he was leaving, she thought. This room was like a secret world. It would never be the same at school.

"Killy, would you go out with me? Next weekend, when I'm better? Maybe we could go to a movie together . . . or play some field hockey." Killy retrieved her hand to stifle a giggle.

"OK. Sure. I'd like to go out with you. But now I've got to get out of here. They'll be bringing your dinner soon."

"Good night, Killy. I'll call you."

"Good night, Tom, Oh, and Tom—" Killy had her hand on the door and suddenly looked very serious. "Work on your Bogart impersonation. Yours was the worst one I've ever heard."

As she darted out of the room, she heard the empty paper cup hit the closed door. She could hear Tom laughing and feel the scowling nurse's eyes following her all the way to the elevator.

The elevator was empty. When the doors slid shut, Killy grinned and did a pirouette.

"I've got a date with Tom!" She closed her eyes, recalling how warm she had felt when Tom held her hand. When she opened her eyes, the doors of the elevator had opened too, and Killy was facing about half a dozen puzzled faces. She walked quickly past them, embarrassed but glowing.

Chapter Four

When Killy thought about her other part-time job she realized how ironic it was. Imagine a future news correspondent delivering newspapers! She liked her job at the hospital, but she hated being a newsgirl five mornings a week. But the money helped out at home, and she wanted to contribute, if only in a small way.

Except for Meg and Carrie, none of the kids at school knew about the newspaper route. Killy wanted to keep it that way. They would only make fun of her more if they knew.

She smiled as she took her bike out of the garage, thinking of how Tom had called her "super sleuth." It was 6 A.M. and cold as she loaded the rolled newspapers into the cloth bag slung over her shoulder. At least, she thought, it was bicycle weather again. In winter she had to make deliveries on foot, which took twice the time.

Today not even the weight of the newspapers could drag down her good spirits. Tonight she was going out with Tom. He had called her twice since she had seen him in the hospital, and he had poked his head into the newsroom several times just to say hello.

At the end of the driveway, Killy looked both ways. The road was empty, as it usually was at this time of day. She pedaled hard as far as the curve and coasted toward the first house. *Thwack* —the paper landed neatly at the top of the front steps. It had become a mechanical action, throwing the papers and hearing them land over and over again. She felt as if she were on automatic pilot.

Her thoughts drifted back to the coming evening. Killy had pretended to her mother, Meg, and Carrie that she couldn't understand the fuss they were making about it. But she really did enjoy the attention. Her mother had questions about Tom: Who was he? What was he like? Was he nice?

Killy hated the word *nice*. It wasn't even strong enough to describe the weather, she thought, let alone a personality. Meg had used it, too, when Killy had told her two friends about Tom.

"Oh, Killy, he's so nice. He was my lab partner first semester. I probably could have gotten interested in him myself, but at the time all I could think about was Andy," Meg said.

Carrie had been happy for Killy, too, but was hurt that Killy hadn't told them about Tom sooner. "You're so mysterious. Honestly, Killy, you never even mentioned seeing Tom in the hospital."

Now as she continued along her route, Killy thought that she hadn't been deliberately mysterious. It had just been difficult to talk about Tom, to reveal her feelings about him. Anyway, what if the whole thing had fizzled? But it hadn't fizzled, and now she finally had a date!

In her excitement Killy was going too fast. The bike was definitely not on automatic pilot! Racing down the hill to her last four deliveries, she saw a huge puddle looming before her. She swerved to avoid it, skidded, and landed on her side. Luckily, the newspapers cushioned her fall. For a moment she was stunned and thought she heard voices.

But it was only one voice she heard—Tom's. He was wearing a blue jogging suit and a neck brace. He stood like a giant over her. "Hey, Killy. Are you all right? Let me give you a hand."

"What are you doing here?" Killy felt wet and cold. Her pale blue jacket was streaked with mud.

"Don't tell my doctor," he said conspiratorially, "but I didn't think it would hurt to do a little jogging. I like coming out at this time of day—no cars to hassle me and usually no runaway bikes."

Tom checked her bike, which appeared undamaged. She checked herself and the newspapers. She was more wet than they were. They could still be delivered. Tom hadn't said anything to make her feel embarrassed, but she still felt stupid standing there, dripping and dirty.

She assured him twice that she was fine but had to get going. "Well, thank you for helping me. I guess I'll see you later—tonight, I mean." Killy felt awkward climbing back on her bike.

"You bet. I'm looking forward to it. Listen, maybe you should be using a car to do this route. You'd probably be safer and you wouldn't get as wet." Tom smiled and waved her off.

A car! Killy was pedaling slowly, but her mind was racing. *He must think I'm old enough to drive! He must not know how young I am. He must not have heard the jokes about me. And now he knows I've got a newspaper route! I've got to talk to him and ask him not to mention it to anyone. Oh, why can't I just have a normal date like anyone else without all these complications?*

The day couldn't go fast enough for Killy. She dashed from the newsroom instead of hanging around as she usually did. At home she showered and washed her hair. She changed clothes three times until she decided on her blue cashmere sweater and tailored tan slacks. At dinner she couldn't eat much. She had had butterflies in her stomach since lunch.

Tom was more relaxed than Killy was when he met her mother. Killy announced she was ready to leave as soon as her mother invited Tom to sit down. He looked from one to the other and smiled. Killy hurried to the door, grabbed a lightweight jacket, and Tom followed, calling goodbye to her mother.

In the car he looked at Killy and laughed. "You were sure in a hurry. Your mom seems nice. Shouldn't you have brought a heavier jacket or something? It's going to get cold later."

"No, I'll be fine. I've also got this warm

sweater on." Killy was waiting for the right opportunity to tell him not to mention the newspaper route.

"That sweater is *also* pretty. It matches your eyes. In fact I've been thinking about your eyes since I picked you out of that puddle this morning. I decided they're sunset blue.

"I like that. No one has ever said that—sunset blue. It sounds poetic." They were stopped for a light, and Killy looked at him and smiled. "There's something I want to tell you . . . or ask you."

"OK if I ask you something first?" He pulled smoothly into the highway traffic. "In all the time we saw each other at the hospital, I never really asked you about yourself. I mean, I got to know you a little, but I never tried to picture where you lived and what your family was like. It was strange picking you up and finding you in a big farmhouse filled with antiques. They are antiques, aren't they?"

"Yes, they're antiques." Killy laughed. "All right. I got to interview you. Now it's your turn, I guess."

"For the record, Miss Wyler, and for our studio audience, would you tell us if there is a big family to go with the big house we have just seen?" Tom had deepened his voice to sound like a typical television news reporter.

They were both laughing now, the way they had at the hospital. "Please! That voice cracks me up. No, there's no big family to go with the big house. It's just my mother and me—my mother is divorced. It's really my grandparents' house." She checked to see if he was still listening. He seemed to be.

"My grandparents lived in the house until I was about five. Then they moved to a farm they bought for their retirement. It was easier and cheaper for my mother to take over their house than to get an apartment. We also ended up with most of their furniture, but that's all right. I like living with things that have some history. What's your house like?"

"Comfortable, but the history only goes back to last summer. My mother decided when we moved that it was time to begin a new life, especially in terms of furniture. She calls it contemporary. I call it—I don't know. You know, I never even thought about it until you started talking about your house. Who started all this, anyway?" Tom threw her a quick glance.

"You did," Killy said, giggling.

"We return now to our regularly scheduled broadcast." He hoped the sudden change in his voice would make her laugh. And he was rewarded.

They talked all the way to the RollerBowl. Tom said he had chosen it because there were no Bogart movies playing in town. Then he told her about his family. He said he was the youngest of three children and the only one still living at home. She liked the way he talked about his parents and his brother and sister. When they left the car and walked across the parking lot to the RollerBowl, Killy shivered. Tom was right. It had already gotten colder.

"Aha! I knew it," Tom said, seeing her shiver. "If you don't watch it, I'll be visiting *you* in the hospital. Here, take my jacket." Despite her protests, he took off his down jacket and put it over her lightweight one. He kept his arm around her shoulder for just a moment. It felt nice— strong and gentle at the same time.

"Shall we roll or bowl?" Tom asked when they were inside. "Do you skate? You decide, Killy."

"Let's put it this way, Tom. You saw me on a bicycle this morning. You know how well I do at sports. I think your neck and I will be safer bowling. After all, I can only hurt the pins."

It took them awhile to find the right ball for her. They finally selected a child's ball. He laughed at her form, a sort of half dance to the throwing line. Then he laughed at himself when she made a strike. They both ended up laughing so much they forgot to keep score and called the game a tie.

The next stop was the Hero Factory. Killy had been there once in the daytime with Meg and Carrie, but at night it looked and sounded completely different. It had been a mill at one time and then a coat factory. Killy thought it looked eerie all lit up at night, like an opening scene from a Frankenstein movie—only with rock music playing in the background. She felt cold until Tom put his arm around her and kept it there until they were inside.

The lights and music hit her at once, and Killy felt dizzy. Tom took her hand to lead her through the crowd. Earlier in the day, she had imagined a table for two in a quiet restaurant, the two of them talking. Not a chance here!

There were two empty chairs at a table of eight, and Killy saw Kim and other friends of Tom's beckoning to him. There was no choice but to sit with them.

Kim ignored Killy. In fact she called her Kelly until Tom corrected her and reminded her that she had known Killy a lot longer than he had. If Kim knew she was being put down, she didn't show it. She flashed a smile and put her arm around Jack Compton's shoulders. Jack was a junior and a friend of Tom's. Killy noticed that Kim was wearing a magenta silk blouse and her usual designer jeans.

"Hey, Tom," called Jack. "I hear you're working at the greenhouse. Dirty job, eh?" Killy thought Kim laughed too hard at this feeble attempt at a joke.

"It's not bad. It's certainly not as rough as Killy's job delivering newspapers." Tom looked at her, but Killy's head was spinning. She couldn't believe Tom had just said that. All she could hear was laughter. Then she heard Kim.

"Why, Killy, you must be competing with my eleven-year-old brother. He's trying to win the ten-speed bike for getting the most subscribers. Or are you trying to win the trip to Washington?" Everyone was laughing now—except for Tom. He was looking at her with concern in his eyes.

"Aren't you going to stick up for yourself, Killy?" he whispered.

"I can't, not now. Please take me home." She felt sick. The lights, the music, the laughter that sounded like a soundtrack from a movie—everything was swirling around in her brain. "Please take me home, Tom," she repeated.

"OK, Killy, I'll take you home," he whispered, but he looked disappointed.

In the car she just sat there, looking straight ahead.

They rode in silence. When Tom eased the car into her driveway, Killy thought of how she had pictured the date would end—with Tom kissing her good night. Instead, as soon as he braked, she ran to the house without looking back.

Inside, even the warmth of the house gave her a chill. Her mother looked up from a book. "Killy, are you all right? What happened?"

"Nothing, Mom, absolutely nothing. I'm fine. I really am. We can talk about it in the morning, OK? I just want to get some rest."

She raced up the stairs to her room and began to undress. Before she could torture herself with the memory of her disastrous first date, she fell into a deep sleep.

Chapter Five

The next morning she awoke with a fever. She had slept for almost twelve hours. When she sat up she was dizzy and fell back on the pillow. Then she slept for another two hours until she felt a hand on her forehead.

"Thank heavens you're cooler now. How do you feel, kiddo?"

Killy had to rub her eyes to get them to focus on her mother. "Awful. Better, but awful. How long have I been asleep? I don't even remember getting into bed last night."

"Well, it's almost noon, and I'm not surprised you don't remember falling asleep. You looked sick last night when you came in. I checked you five minutes after you went upstairs and you were already in a deep sleep. Did your stomach hurt at all?"

"It didn't really hurt, but it started feeling kind of funny at lunch yesterday."

"That's what Dr. Sabella thought. I called him this morning, and he guessed it was the flu. He said there had been about thirty cases of it reported to his office this week. You should be feeling better this afternoon. If not, he wants to see you." Her mother straightened the quilt on the bed and put on a fresh pillowcase.

"I don't feel dizzy anymore, and I think I could eat something. Were you up all night with me? You look tired."

"Don't worry. I got some sleep. I just checked you a few times during the night. Tell you what! Let's start with the tea and toast treatment. If that sits well, you can have something more later today. Why don't you go wash your face, and I'll serve you up here, madame."

After the tea and two slices of toast, Killy was better—still weak but more herself again. "I think I'll get dressed and come downstairs."

"No way! Stay in bed until dinner at least. Then if you want to move around, come down and stretch out on the sofa. I'll make us dinner on trays, and we can watch an old movie while we eat."

Killy reluctantly agreed. She hated being in bed and was restless. Most of all, she did not want to think about last night. "Could I have a book? I wish I had a telephone by the bed. Maybe I'll go over to the desk and work on my project."

Her mother grabbed a small pillow from the window seat and aimed for Killy's head. "You have always been a terrible patient." She laughed. "I guess I should be grateful this is only one of those twenty-four-hour deals. It better be! Remember when you were six and had the bad sore throat? I tucked you in to sleep one day and half an hour later found you out trying to ride your bike. Some things never change! Now be good or I won't give you the good news."

She went along with her mother's teasing. "OK, I promise. I'll stay in bed until dinner. But tell me the good news now, or I'll start turning cartwheels around the room."

"It's a deal. Your Aunt Jill is in Boston today on a business trip, and she's going to drive down to spend the day with us tomorrow."

"Mom, that's great. We haven't seen her since before Christmas. I want to hear about every place she's been. Someday I'm going to travel, just like Aunt Jill."

"Right now, you'd better settle for a book.

Is this the one you want?" Killy nodded and took the book from her mother. It was a novel about an art student, set in Venice, Italy.

When her mother left, she opened the book and started at the first page without reading. She kept repeating the same words in her mind, over and over! *I will not think about last night.* But it didn't work. How could she forget the most humiliating night of her life? How could she forget that Tom had been there and seen what a baby she really was? And how could any girl forget that the first date she had dreamed of for so long had probably destroyed her social life forever?

Jill Killgore never walked into a room. She breezed in. Her energy and enthusiasm could be felt even before she spoke. Killy and her mother were usually overwhelmed at first but quickly got caught up in Jill's high spirits.

"Killy, you're gorgeous! Prettier than the last time I saw you. I told you she was going to look like Leslie Caron some day, Kate, and she's almost there." Jill gave her niece a long hug.

As always, Aunt Jill had a present for each of them, and as always, Killy's mother protested that it was not necessary to bring a present every time she visited. Still, her mother had opened her present before Killy could even get the paper off her own.

"Jill, where did you find this? It's antique, but it has my initials on it." Her mother showed Killy the delicately scrolled silver napkin ring.

"Wait until Killy opens hers, and then I'll tell you." From a mountain of tissue and newspaper, Killy lifted out a small teapot covered with pink and violet flowers.

"Thank you, Aunt Jill! Let's use it today. Does it have a history?"

"I don't know about the history. Actually, the teapot was going to be for the both of you. But while it was being wrapped, I started rummaging through a box of napkin rings. I think I shrieked when I saw one with your initials, Kate. Naturally I couldn't leave it there, so I bought it! Hmm . . . let's give the teapot a history. I say it belonged to a wealthy Beacon Hill family. Your turn, Kate."

"It was willed to a faithful, long-serving maid, who was forced to sell it to support her ailing daughter who was always coming down with the flu." They were all laughing now. It was Killy's turn.

"It was located in an antique shop by a dear woman who purchased it for her darling niece. The niece, being a clever girl, immediately recognized the pot as one brought over on the *Mayflower*. Her wealth was assured, and she would never have to work. Instead, she would travel with her mother and aunt all over the world." They laughed, pleased with the history they had created.

"Is your daughter often this far up in the clouds?" Jill said teasingly. "If she's that excited over a teapot, do you suppose I should hold off telling her what we discussed?" The two women grinned at each other, and Killy thought she would burst if they kept it up any longer.

"What did you discuss? Tell me!"

"It's your graduation present." Her aunt knew Killy was about to interrupt and continued quickly. "I know it's a year or so early, but this is sort of a now-or-never gift. How would you like to spend your spring break in Italy—Florence, to be exact—with me and my old school friend, Andrea?"

It was too much for Killy to take in all at once. She was speechless. It was unreal, but she knew what she just heard was true!

"You really mean it? You want to take me with you to Italy? Me? Aunt Jill, I can't believe it! Can I go, Mom?" Killy's words were tumbling out. Her mother and aunt were laughing so hard that tears were rolling down their cheeks. Killy was laughing now, too, and twirling about the room.

"Kate," Jill said, "I'm glad I don't have to live with this for the next month. You won't have a moment's peace with her dancing around."

For the rest of the day, and until it was time for Jill to return to Boston, the talk was only of Italy. Killy managed to calm down enough to discuss the details. They would be staying with Jill's friend, Andrea. Jill had met Andrea when she had studied for a year in Florence. Since then, they had kept up their friendship. Staying with Andrea would be fun, Jill said. And the apartment was convenient to all the sightseeing and shopping areas they'd want to visit. She even suggested books on Florence that Killy might want to read before the trip.

By the time they waved Jill down the driveway, Killy and her mother looked exhausted from the excitement. They walked arm in arm back to the house. Later, they decided to go to the Italian restaurant in town to celebrate. Killy's appetite had recovered enough for her to eat a plate of spaghetti with clam sauce and half a loaf of garlic bread.

In the middle of dessert, she started thinking about Tom for the first time that day. Even her exciting new plans could not make her memories of the date less painful, so she quickly thought of a question to ask her mother about the trip. Soon they were deep in conversation, and her painful thoughts were driven away for the moment.

Chapter Six

Killy had never felt so torn in her life. On the one hand, she couldn't wait to see Meg and Carrie to tell them about the trip. On the other hand, she knew that what they'd really want to know about was her date with Tom. And what could she tell them? Maybe they already knew the whole terrible story. Maybe Kim had already spread the word. In that case, how could she face even her best friends? How could her life be so wonderful and awful at the same time?

So she didn't call either of her friends over the weekend. And when the three of them met at the foot of Carrie's driveway on Monday morning for their customary walk to school, Meg and Carrie were dying of curiosity.

"Killy, how was Friday night? Why didn't

you call me right away? Where were you last night when I tried to call you? Did you have a good time? Did he ask you out again? Why are you being so secretive about all this?" That was nonstop Carrie.

"Hi, Killy. How was your weekend?" Meg asked politely, but she had a twinkle in her eye.

"Listen, you guys, give me a break. I've got something much more exciting to tell you about than a silly date."

Meg and Carrie stared at each other in disbelief. "Killy, what in the world are you talking about?" Carrie asked.

But her reaction to Killy's news was immediate. As soon as she heard where Killy was going, she said, "Italy! Killy, you've got to be the luckiest person I know! Spring vacation in Italy, and I've never been anywhere." Carrie flung out one arm in an emotional gesture and almost dropped her books.

"You went to Florida last year and California the year before that," Meg calmly reminded her. "I think it sounds really exciting, Killy," she added.

"You know what I mean, Meg," Carrie continued. "I've never been anywhere you need a passport to get to—any place foreign. Meg, I really don't understand you sometimes. How can you be so calm about this? You still look like Mary what's-her-name you played in the Drama Club play last year."

"Mary Queen of Scots. And, of course, I'm excited for Killy. Actually, I was thinking about what I've read of Florence and wondering if the medieval presence can still be felt." At that, both Killy and Carrie started to laugh.

"Honestly, Meg, I don't believe you!" Carrie said. "You're thinking medieval, and I'm thinking Italian silk scarves and leather handbags and shoes and gorgeous men with Roman noses and—"

"I'm going to Florence, Carrie, not Rome."

"Well, men with Florentine noses! What's the difference? They're still Italian men and very romantic." As an afterthought to Meg, Carrie added, "At least from what I've read."

Killy was used to smoothing over their disagreements. "Look, I'm glad you're both excited for me. I'm counting on both of you to help me get ready for this trip. I don't even know what the weather will be like. I'm going to the library this afternoon to check out some travel books."

"I'll check the city paper for you every day for the 'Temperatures Abroad' column. That will give you an idea of what to bring with you." Meg was definitely concentrating on Killy's coming trip.

"Library! Someone said 'library.'" Now it was Carrie who was concentrating.

"That was half a block ago. I said I was going to the library this afternoon," Killy reminded her.

Carrie sped off, calling over her shoulder, "I've got to return these books before first period. They're two weeks overdue. See you." Her auburn hair flying and her long mohair scarf dancing in the wind, Carrie quickly became a blur of color in the distance.

Good. They forgot about Tom, Killy thought. But she was not going to be let off so easily.

She and Meg walked in silence for a while, watching Carrie disappear from view. "Are you going to tell me about your date with Tom Friday night?" Meg asked quietly.

"There isn't really much to tell," Killy said.

"Oh, Killy, please tell me what happened. I can tell something's wrong."

Killy looked at her friend and tried not to cry. "I made a complete fool of myself. That's what happened. Tom will never want to see me again."

"Killy, will you just tell me what happened? It can't have been *that* bad."

"Well, it started out all right. But then we went to the Hero Factory, and Kim and her friends were there."

"So?"

"Well, someone was talking about jobs, and before I could stop Tom, he blurted out something about my newspaper route. You can imagine what Kim did with that piece of news."

"Oh, Killy, that must have been awful. Kim teases you about your age enough anyway. But I hope you didn't take any grief from her."

"Meg, I was so embarrassed I didn't know what to do. Besides, I was coming down with the flu at the time. So I just sat there like an idiot, and then finally I begged Tom to take me home, just like a little kid. We didn't say a word all the way home, and I'm sure he'll never speak to me again as long as I live."

"Oh, Killy, I'm so sorry. But I'm sure you're wrong about Tom. Try to give him a little credit. I'm sure he knows what Kim is like and how you must feel. You've just got to learn how to handle that girl."

"Well, I'm sure Tom isn't interested in sticking around and waiting for me to grow up. How can I ever face him again? How could this have happened to me on my very first date?"

"Killy, things will work out. I just know they will."

"You do not, Meg. You don't know anything about it, so stop trying to make me feel good." Her friend looked so hurt, Killy said, "I'm sorry. Let's not talk about it anymore, OK?"

"OK, if that's what you want."

"Friends?"

Meg nodded and continued walking, her chin held high.

"You know you *do* look like Mary Queen of Scots when you walk that way."

"Actually, I'm trying to get into character as Joan of Arc. The Drama Club is doing that in May, and I want the lead."

"Will you have to cut your hair if you get the part?" Meg had beautiful long black hair.

"I just might."

The girls looked at each other and grinned. Killy assumed Meg's style of walking, and together they looked as if they were leading an army into the school.

*   *   *

If Carrie had run to school early to return books, she also used the time to spread the news of Killy's trip. By the time Killy reached her locker, she thought half the school must know that she was going to Italy. The reaction was a mixture of good-natured envy and enthusiasm, and Killy glowed with the attention just as she had the day she had won the journalism award.

"Italy?" Killy could hear Kim talking to the other girls. "How enriching . . . all those statues and ruins. But where will she find another *child* to take over her newspaper route?" There was some giggling, but Killy didn't turn to look. Instead she continued trying to fit her gym clothes into her locker, which was rapidly filling with plants and roots for her chemistry project.

"Here. You dropped this." Tom handed Killy a sneaker, which looked old and ugly in his hand. Killy grabbed it and threw it in the locker, quickly shutting the door before the shoe could fall out again.

"I want to talk to you, Killy. I was going to call you over the weekend, but I thought I'd rather see you in person." He looked serious, and Killy was afraid to hear what he had to say.

"I'm sorry, Tom, I don't have much time right now. I have to get to homeroom."

"I didn't mean now. Something happened the other night that I don't understand, and I think we should talk about it."

Killy cut him off. "I know you didn't know how old I was when you asked me out. That's my fault. I should have told you and given you a chance to back out. Don't worry, it's all right. You don't have to let me down easy now. I understand how you feel."

"Killy, stop finishing sentences for me and let me say what I want." Tom's voice was tense. "Will you meet me after school?"

"Listen, I've got to run. And after school I have to get to the library downtown and do some research. I'm going to Italy on spring break, and there's so much—"

Now he cut her off. "Do you know what? You're really acting like a baby now."

It was all she had to hear. Her locker door had popped open again, and this time she slammed it so hard that it made the whole line of lockers vibrate. With the sound ringing in her ears, she turned and ran down the hall.

Inside her homeroom, she tried to get control of herself. She took a deep breath and swallowed it away. *I am not going to cry. I am not going to let any of this get me down. Not now. Not when I'm going to Italy. For once, I'll be someplace where I won't have to think about kids like Kim and about newspaper deliveries. Maybe I'll even forget about Tom.*

She stared straight ahead as the morning announcements were read over the loudspeaker.

Chapter Seven

The next few weeks sped by for Killy. Tom didn't try to see her again, and she was *almost* too busy to think about him. She went on shopping trips with her mother, got endless tips from Carrie on how to look and act sophisticated to attract European men, and spent hours with Meg pouring over books on the art treasures of Florence.

But none of the travel and art books she looked at quite prepared her for her first view of Florence. She and her aunt arrived late at night, and the ride to Andrea's apartment revealed not much more than a blur of lights as the taxi whizzed through the streets. But in the morning, when she threw open the dark green shutters of her bedroom, Killy raised the curtain on a spectacular scene. The city outside was a living, glossy photograph in shades of red and gold.

The stretch of red tile roofs and honey-colored buildings below was interrupted at points by vast towers and domes that she couldn't wait to explore.

"Aunt Jill, Andrea!" Killy dashed through the apartment and found her aunt in the kitchen opening cupboard after cupboard.

"Andrea's not here. She's at work. Unfortunately, she has only five days' vacation time while we're here. Today's not one of them. What's the emergency? You came in here like someone was chasing you."

"It's so exciting! I've been staring at everything I can see from my window and listening to the sounds, and I've got to get out and be part of it. Let's go right away, OK?"

Her aunt grinned. "Don't you think we should at least get dressed first? Actually, we should go out. I can't find anything to eat or even where Andrea hides the coffee. What did you think of my friend from your quick meeting last night?"

"I like her. But she's not at all what I expected. The two of you are so different. You're so tall and fair and outgoing. And Andrea's so tiny and not shy exactly—but quiet, if you know what I mean. It's hard to imagine the two of you friends, but then sometimes it's hard to imagine what Meg and Carrie and I have in common, too. Oh, I don't know what I'm talking about. Let's just get outside! I'm so excited I can't stand it."

"OK, let's go. We'll grab something at a bar, do some sightseeing, and pick up some groceries."

Killy looked puzzled at the word "bar" until her aunt explained that in Florence it meant a stand-up lunch counter. Five minutes later, Killy had thrown on a blue T-shirt and her wrap-around skirt and was pacing in the living room waiting for her aunt. At the call of "Let's go," she was out the door and in the hallway.

The bright sun made Killy blink as she emerged from the building's small lobby. She looked in the direction of the river and was ready to dart into the street.

"Hold on, honey. You're taking your life in your hands trying to get this traffic to stop for you. We'll keep walking until there's a break. Besides, there's a bar a few doors up, and I really think we should eat first. I'll be able to handle your enthusiasm a little better when I've had my coffee!" Jill grabbed her niece's arm and steered her up the avenue.

It was follow the leader for the rest of the day, with Killy doing the following. For one thing, most of the sidewalks were so narrow that it was impossible for the two of them to walk side by side. For another, her aunt was pretty excited, too, to be back in this city that she really loved. She kept racing ahead to get to places she had missed all the years she'd been away.

At one point Jill almost lost her niece. They were walking across the Ponte Vecchio, an ancient bridge of stores spanning the Arno River. Killy suddenly looked down at the cobblestones and stopped. She remembered reading that this very bridge was on the route Michelangelo used to reach his workshop centuries ago. This was more than just seeing history, it was touching it, and Killy felt a chill go down her spine as she stood there.

Halfway across the bridge, Killy saw her aunt up ahead, waving frantically to her. In an instant Killy left the sixteenth century and was back in the present.

"Hey! How about letting me know when you're stopping?" Jill was smiling, so Killy knew she wasn't really angry.

"Oh, Aunt Jill. I still can't believe I'm really

here—really a part of all this. Thank you so much for bringing me here. I promise I won't be any trouble."

"You're not any trouble to me, Killy. Seeing you here and watching how thrilled you are makes me know I made the right decision." She put her arm around Killy's shoulders. "Come on, let's start back."

"Already? But there's so much to see!"

"If you're going to live here awhile, you'd better learn to—pardon the joke—do as the Florentines do. After lunch, and until about four o'clock, the city rests. You'll see that most of the shops close up in the heat of the day and reopen later. You can sleep or read, but in an hour or so, about the only people you'll see outdoors are the tourists!"

"Well, that will take some getting used to, but I definitely don't want to look like a tourist." Killy and her aunt exchanged glances and then laughed.

At the apartment Jill made lunch. Killy watched as she deep-fried slivers of zucchini in bubbling oil. Then Killy began wolfing them down like potato chips. They were delicious!

"Hold it! We also have cheese and bread and those big oranges we bought." Jill started slicing a round, crusty loaf of bread, and Killy unwrapped the wedge of cheese.

"Do you always eat this way?" Killy asked.

"Only in Italy. At home, I'd probably be eating a container of yogurt if I were on my diet. Otherwise, I'd be out eating a giant cheeseburger."

Over lunch, Killy and Jill talked as though they were getting to know each other for the first time. Killy asked her aunt about her job with an international investment banking firm and about the year she had spent in Florence when she was in college. And Jill asked her about life in Ridgefield and her friends.

"There's not much to tell. I wrote you about winning the journalism award, and I've told you about my best friends, Meg and Carrie. Carrie, by the way, would not settle for this kind of lunch or anything less than a whole pizza. She was a vegetarian for exactly thirteen days until we passed one of those burger-a-second places. You could see the steam pouring out of a pipe on the roof and smell the burgers from a block away. That did it! She ran in and ordered one with everything on it."

Jill was laughing and trying to section her orange with one eye closed in case some juice squirted out. "That's funny. I remember Carrie.

You went to a party at her house. You wrote me about it."

"Aunt Jill, it wasn't a real party. It was just a sleep-over with Carrie, Meg, and me. The highlight was when Carrie painted Meg's toenails purple."

"Come on, Killy, you must go to *other* parties with boys."

"Sorry to disappoint you, Aunt Jill, but you've got the wrong idea. If you think I'm invited to a party a week or that boys are lined up at the door, then you have more imagination than Mom says *I* have."

Jill's face registered her surprise. "But you're so bright and pretty. I can't understand why you're not one of the most popular girls at school."

"Thanks for the compliment. I wish I had as much confidence in my looks as you do. Anyway, at my school, being pretty or bright doesn't count as much as how well you flirt. And don't forget, all through school I've had this label of 'baby' hanging over me."

"I can see how that might be a problem with some of the kids. But you're so mature, I can't believe your age really matters that much. Who you are is what's important, you know."

"But people are always teasing me about

my age, and I don't know how to handle it. In grade school I was proud of skipping two grades, but now I wish I hadn't."

"Look, Killy, how many kids actually tease you? A few? A dozen? Just don't waste your time on them." She handed Killy a section of orange. "And don't give up on everyone else or you're going to miss out on a lot of fun. Anyway, I think you're going to love your two weeks in Italy. Andrea said she's going to have her cousin Fabrio take you out and meet his friends."

Andrea walked in the door just as Killy was choking on her orange. "You arranged a date for me? Forget it. I don't need anyone to take me out. I've got a whole city to explore, and the museums alone will probably take the rest of the vacation."

Hearing Killy's reaction startled Andrea. "Why, Killy, you will get to see everything you want, but there are evenings also. I thought you would be happy meeting people your own age."

"Andrea's right, Killy. I don't want you to feel tied to me. You'd feel out of place with my friends. I don't want you to be bored."

"I'm sorry, Andrea and Aunt Jill. I didn't mean to snap at you or sound ungrateful. It's just that I'm used to spending evenings at home, and I don't really mind it. You didn't have to go out of your way."

"I didn't go out of my way," Andrea said, and smiled. "Perhaps you will enjoy meeting Fabrio, perhaps not. Why don't you wait and see?"

"She's right, Killy. You don't have to spend any time with him. It's your decision. But at least give it a try, OK? Now, do you want to spend your time with us? I'll probably doze when Andrea goes back to work."

"I really am tired. I won't sleep, but maybe I'll just stretch out." Killy left her aunt and Andrea looking over a concert schedule. With her glasses on and her blond hair pulled tightly back into a knot, her aunt looked like a model for a businesswoman's magazine, Killy thought. And Andrea looked just like a little kid, grinning above her orange.

In her room, Killy looked out the window. All the green shutters across the street that had been open this morning were now shut tight. Killy drew hers closed too, and the room was instantly cooler. She thought about writing a postcard but instead stretched out on the bed.

I'll try to go along with it for their sake, she thought, as she studied the cracks in the ceiling. *But I just know this is going to be a disaster. I had enough trouble at home going out on a date and trying to fit in with a group. If things were that bad in English, I hate to think of what it's going to be like in Italian!*

The last thought Killy had before she fell asleep was that the cracks in the ceiling looked like the branches of the apple tree at home.

Chapter Eight

"Killy, Killy, wake up! This was a siesta, not the Rip Van Winkle competition." Jill was sitting on the bed, and for a moment Killy couldn't remember where she was. But when her aunt opened the shutters to the soft glow of the afternoon, Killy was wide awake.

"I'm sorry. Did I oversleep?" Killy sat up and pushed the hair from her face.

"No, you didn't oversleep. We're not on a schedule here, but I knew you wouldn't want to miss sightseeing this afternoon."

"I'll be ready in a minute. Where are we going?"

"You're on your own. I'm going to the university. I've got friends I went to school with who are now instructors—if you can believe people being *that* old—and one who's a professor. Andrea is meeting us there after work, and we're all going to dinner."

Killy must have looked slightly helpless, for her aunt said, "Killy, you'll do fine on your own. I've got a map for you, but I don't think you'll need it. No matter where you go, just head back toward the river and follow it. There may be kids at home who think you're a baby, but I don't. You're more mature than I was at your age. And that's not easy to admit!"

"Well, I do want to see the cathedral—the Duomo. Is that on the map?"

"I'm not laughing at you, Killy, but believe me, you can't miss the cathedral. Remember the street of shops we were on this morning? Keep heading up that street and when you see the cathedral, you'll know why I laughed. Remember to tell me tonight your first impression. Now I've got to get going. There's enough food here for dinner. Sorry to leave you alone your first day. We'll spend more time together tomorrow, okay? Have a good time."

Jill gave Killy a quick kiss and left, closing the door behind her.

The afternoon was an adventure Killy would never forget. She stood on the Ponte Vecchio again, this time leaning leisurely over the wall of the bridge and watching her reflection in the shimmering water below. Crossing a wide avenue after leaving the bridge was an adventure in itself, and Killy believed she would never have made it through the honking cars without the help of a kind policeman. He stood on an island in the middle of the avenue, waving his arms like a symphony conductor and made a sweeping bow as he let Killy pass to the opposite side.

In a picturesque outdoor café with tables covered by cool blue-and-white umbrellas, Killy made her first efforts to speak Italian.

"*Buona sera, signorina.*" The smiling waiter had a mustache that stretched from ear to ear.

"*Buona sera,*" Killy said in what she thought was a pretty good imitation of an Italian accent. She quickly hunted in her Italian-English dictionary for the word *lemonade.*

"*Una limonata, pia—*" She couldn't remember the word for "please."

"*Piacere?*"

"*Sì,*" she said, smiling back at him.

"*Limonata, cola, caffè, aranciata . . .*" He had been through this before, Killy thought, and she laughed.

"*Una limonata,*" she repeated.

"*Si! Una limonata,*" the waiter responded, and Killy sighed in relief.

After finishing her lemonade and resting her feet, which was her real reason for stopping at the café, Killy followed a stream of pedestrians who were zigzagging through the narrow streets. She knew the cathedral was in the center of the city, and she hoped the people she was following were headed there. Killy kept her eyes on the street, watching her footing on the cobblestones, and when she looked up, there it was. The cathedral! Then she understood why her aunt had laughed. It was impossible to miss the massive marble cathedral.

Her eyes couldn't take it in all at once. Slowly she scanned the facade. Neck arched, she gazed at the great dome until she felt stiff and then turned to look at the soaring bell tower. At eye level and facing the cathedral she spotted the Baptistry, a small octagonal building. She remembered her aunt mentioning that she must see the bronze doors of the Baptistery. But the traffic in the square surrounding the cathedral and the crowds of tourists clustered around the Baptistery convinced Killy that she should wait for another day to see the famous doors.

*　　*　　*

Finding her way back to the apartment was as uncomplicated as her aunt had promised. With only one wrong turn, Killy found her way. Home at last, all she wanted to do was take a hot shower and collapse.

She got into her white terry robe, and two minutes later turned on the shower. When the water was finally beating on her tired muscles, Killy guessed that she must have walked five miles or more that day.

Suddenly she realized that the doorbell was ringing. She grabbed her robe and rushed to the door, thinking that her aunt must have forgotten something.

"Aunt Jill, what did—" Killy opened the door to a handsome but serious-looking young man with dark hair and brown eyes. He was dressed very formally in a blue blazer and gray slacks.

"Fabrio," he said extending his hand. "Fabrio Novelli. And you, I am sure, are Killy."

The water was running off her hair and down her face. "Oh, yes. My aunt said—Do you speak English?"

"Yes, I speak English, which is fortunate for you because I do not imagine you speak Italian." He let himself into the apartment.

"Well, I've been using my dictionary and studying a language book. But wait a minute!

What are you doing here now? I thought Andrea would be here when I met you."

He studied her a moment, and Killy felt uncomfortable standing in her robe with her hair dripping into her collar. "Andrea did not tell you I would be arriving?"

"Yes, she told me, but she didn't say when."

"Then you knew I was coming. That is fine. I thought tonight we could eat at my favorite café and then go to a concert at the Boboli Gardens." He turned and sat in the white armchair. "I will wait while you get dressed."

He was so matter-of-fact. *He must hate this as much as I do*, Killy thought. Her mind was racing. Did she have to ask Aunt Jill for permission to go out for the evening? What should she wear? Should she tell him he didn't have to do this?

In her bedroom she took out the pale blue shirtdress her mother had given her as a going-away present. As she dressed, she mumbled to herself, "I'm doing this for Aunt Jill and Andrea." Her hair was still damp from the shower, so she quickly brushed it straight back, knowing it would fall into her face later when it dried. After a quick, final check in the mirror, she headed for the living room. Fabrio was reading one of Andrea's Italian newsmagazines.

"That is better," he said as he looked up at her. "I mean, your hair is so much more becoming pulled back from your face. Come, we will go." Killy had the impression he was being paid to take her out. She scribbled a hurried note to her aunt as Fabrio stood holding the door open.

Out on the avenue he turned to look at her. "Would you like to cross to the other side and see the river?"

"I was looking at the river just this morning from the Ponte Vecchio. It was beautiful, and I could see my reflection in the water."

Fabrio looked surprised and showed a hint of a smile. "I did not think most tourists took the time to stand and watch the river. Do you know that the average tourist spends only three days in Florence? They shop, go to one or two museums, visit the cathedral, and line up for a brief glimpse of the bronze doors."

"That's why I didn't get to see the doors today. There must have been a hundred or more people around. I can wait. I'd rather go when it's not so crowded."

"I like that, Killy. It is good to take your time." He smiled at her—a wider one than before. Killy thought he was even more handsome when he smiled.

The café Fabrio chose was the same one Killy had visited earlier in the afternoon, the Café Fiona. The waiter was the one who had served her the lemonade that afternoon. This time he greeted her like an old friend. Fabrio was definitely impressed.

"You have already discovered my favorite café and know Angelo, the waiter." Killy could sense his mood changing. He was beginning to show a glimmer of warmth, to which she responded.

He watched her watching the passing parade of people. "I must tell you something," he said. "I really did not want to take you out. I did it for Andrea as a favor."

Killy stopped watching the passersby and looked straight at him. "That makes two of us. I didn't want to come either." They glared at each other and then grinned simultaneously.

"You *are* different, Killy. You know, until we crossed to the river from your apartment, I had one opinion of American teenagers: they stick together, eat at the American bar—'hamwiches' or whatever they call those meat rounds—or sit in the café near the American Express office and return to their 'English spoken here' hotels!"

"Am I to take all this as a compliment?"

"Yes, you should. Anyone who takes the time to study the river is definitely different. And that makes you interesting. And I like that. I think I am going to enjoy this evening."

"I think I'll reserve my opinion until after the concert."

"You see, you are funny. You make me laugh. Now I am going to let you in on my favorite dessert, tiny hot pastries made with rice. I will order some for us when we finish our pasta."

After leaving the Fiona, there was more than an hour to spare before the concert would begin. "Come, there is a church I want to show you. It is not as grand as the cathedral, but I think you will like it." Fabrio guided Killy through the streets, pointing out sights that he thought might interest her. She felt more comfortable with him now, since they both had confessed how reluctant they had been to go out with each other.

They were walking through an open marketplace where vendors with carts were selling everything from watermelons to walking shorts. It was fascinating but hectic and crowded, and she let Fabrio take her arm to guide her through.

One block away was a haven from the noise and chaos, a large piazza with a beautiful church.

"Here we are. This is the church of Santa Maria Novella. My family lived near here when I was a boy, and my mother brought me here almost every day to play by the fountain over there—and sometimes in it." Killy smiled and could almost picture him falling into the fountain.

Fabrio took Killy by the arm. "Let's go inside," he said. As they entered, the church bells began to ring. Inside, Killy studied each stained-glass window and the beautiful frescoes.

"I am glad you like the church. I can tell that you do by the way you look at it. I do not come here as often as I would like. Maybe I have been too busy with school and working to enjoy my own city. Showing you Florence would be fun for me. Would you let me do that while you are here?"

Killy hesitated, and Fabrio spoke again before she could. "Well, you don't have to answer now. We should start for the concert. By the time we reach the Boboli Gardens, it will be almost dark, and the music will begin as soon as the first star is out."

Fabrio found a shortcut back to the Arno River, and soon they were crossing the Ponte Vecchio. It was growing dark, and the lights from the bridge and others from nearby buildings danced on the glassy, black river. The change in the view from earlier in the day was dramatic, and Killy couldn't decide which she liked best.

By the time they were strolling down the gravel path leading to the patio in the gardens, the orchestra was warming up. Fabrio found two seats in the back row, and the music began. Killy looked up at the sky. It was made-to-order navy blue, beautifully clear and studded with a thousand stars. The atmosphere made her feel dreamy and relaxed.

It wasn't until the final applause that she realized Fabrio was lightly squeezing her hand. "You have been far away. Did you enjoy the concert?"

She retrieved her hand, pretending to hunt for a tissue. "Yes, it was lovely . . . perfect. I didn't recognize half of what was being played, but it was all so peaceful. I imagined these gardens were mine and I was walking through them wearing a flowing gown." Killy didn't worry about whether Fabrio would find her ramblings silly or girlish.

"I have an idea that you are a writer from the way you observe and imagine," he said. Then he took her arm and guided her back toward the path, but she moved ahead of him down the aisle, unassisted.

When they were out of the gardens and back on the sidewalk along the river, Fabrio put his arm around her waist. "You are wonderful to be with, Killy," he whispered.

Killy pulled away from him, walked to the wall paralleling the avenue, and looked down at the river.

"Why did you pull away from me? Did you not enjoy today? I did, and I hope we have more good days together while you are in Florence." Fabrio looked confused.

"I have had a good time, and I thank you for everything. But that's all. OK?"

"What is all? I do not understand."

"I just don't want anything serious to start. I'd like to be friends, but if that isn't enough for you—well. . . ." Killy kept her voice low but firm.

"What makes you so frightened of me? I touch you, and you jump. Look at me and tell me what is the matter."

Her eyes continued to study the black river. "It's not just your hand on me. It's what that leads to. And I told you I'm not interested in being serious with anyone."

"Serious? Is that what you think? *You* are the one who is too serious. You misunderstand a gesture from a friend. You seem to enjoy so much about life, and yet you are in such control of yourself that you are missing out on experiencing wonderful feelings—feelings that you will never discover in your imagination or your writing."

Fabrio threw up his hands in a gesture of frustration, then folded his arms and stared at the ground. "I am saying these things to you because I feel I got to know you today, and I found you to be a very special person. Do you know that I never took another girl to my favorite church, but I took you there because I knew you would like it, too. Do you understand anything I am saying?"

She had taken in everything he said, and now her head was swimming, trying to sort out her thoughts. Suddenly she buried her head in her hands and began to sob. She was thinking about her feelings for Fabrio and her feelings for Tom. She was thinking about what had happened to her mother and wondering what in the world was happening to her, Killy. Was she finally starting to grow up?

Then suddenly she felt warm. Fabrio had put his arms around her, and she didn't pull away. When she looked up at him, he was smiling down at her and brushing back her hair with a gentle touch.

"Oh, Killy. You have cried and let a friend hold you. Silly Killy, there *is* hope for you, after all."

Chapter Nine

"I wonder if we shouldn't be filing written reports to keep each other posted on our activities." Jill was teasing, but it was true that she and Killy had not seen much of each other during their vacation. Jill poured coffee for herself and juice for Killy. On the table there were a plate of rolls, a dish of sweet butter curls, and another of marmalade.

"Can you believe how fast the time has gone? I've never had fun like I'm having here. All the things Fabrio and I have done—I kept meaning to write them down, but I've been too busy."

"Tell me more about what you've been doing. You've probably seen more of this city than I did in my first six months of school."

"Well, we went on a picnic in a little village

north of here called Fiesole. The fun of being with Fabrio is that I never know where we're going. He always surprises me. And sometimes even *he* has no idea about what we will do. The other day we drove all over the city making deliveries for his mother's dress shop, in the old city, in the market districts. I really felt part of the city, not just a visitor."

"Did you get to see Fabrio's mother's dress shop?"

"Yes, it's beautiful, more like someone's living room than a store." Killy licked the dripping marmalade from her roll.

"It's one of the most elegant dress shops in Florence, and unfortunately always out of my price range," Jill said, frowning.

"You just reminded me of something." Killy sprang from her chair, taking her roll with her. "Today I *do* know where we're going, and I don't have anything that's right to wear."

"Hold on! First tell me where and then why your clothes won't do. I already know the *who*, and that's got to be Fabrio."

"Fabrio's mother is doing a fashion show tomorrow at a villa just outside the city. Today we're going to bring a vanload of dresses there, and he'll supervise the setting up of chairs and lighting—things like that." Killy was racing to get the words out.

"Sounds like you need work clothes to me."

"Oh, no, Aunt Jill. We'll be working in an ancient villa that overlooks Florence. Fabrio said that it's full of beautiful, original frescoes and magnificent furniture. He promised we could go through most of the rooms and walk in the gardens. For a setting like that, I wanted to look special. And this is my last full day with Fabrio before we have to leave, and I wanted—" She didn't know how to finish the sentence, but Jill caught her meaning, anyway.

"Do you know you look happier and prettier than I've ever seen you? You're even wearing your hair a new way, pulled back from your face. It suits you."

"I *feel* happy. Sometimes I wish we didn't have to leave at all." Killy smiled to herself, thinking of how many good things had happened to her since she came to Italy. Ridgefield seemed years as well as miles away.

"Can I assume that pleased look you're wearing lately has something to do with Fabrio? You do like him, don't you? At first, I was afraid Andrea and I had made a mistake arranging for you to meet him."

"Of course, I like him. But we're just good

friends. There's no involvement or anything."
Killy dug into her roll.

"Who said anything about involvements? Did he?"

"No."

"Then I don't understand."

"I guess I say that automatically when it comes to boys. I'm thinking of Mom, I suppose."

"What about your mother?" Jill's expression had changed, and her tone was serious.

"Oh, nothing. I don't know why I said that."

"I don't know what you're thinking about your mother, but I can guess from what you just said about boys and involvements. I'm going to tell you something, but then I want you to do some serious thinking and talk to your mother when you get back home."

Jill caught her breath and continued. "Listen, Killy, your mother and father were very much in love when they got married. But it just didn't work out. They were both too young, and they were the first to admit that. But your mother has never looked upon what happened as a mistake because it gave her *you*. And if you think hiding *your* feelings can protect you from all life's complications, then you're wrong. You're—oh, I don't know."

Killy sat quietly until her aunt spoke again,

breaking the tension that filled the room. "I'm sorry. I didn't mean to sound angry, but it worries me to think of what's going on inside that head of yours. Just promise me that you'll think about what I've said." Jill came over to Killy and stroked the back of her hair. "Now let's go and figure out something special for you to wear today."

What Jill ended up doing was letting Killy borrow one of her dresses. It was a lime green, wraparound dress with navy blue trim. She helped Killy brush her hair and then gave her two combs to wear on the sides. When Killy looked at herself in the mirror, she felt like a model waiting for the photographers to start snapping away. And when Fabrio picked her up in the van outside Andrea's building, he was beaming.

"Killy, you look wonderful—*bellissima*! There is definitely something different about you today, but I do not know what it is."

She felt terrific as she sat back and enjoyed the view outside her window.

"You never get tired of looking out the window, do you? Even if we have been on this street many times in the last two weeks, I have a feeling you always see something new. That has been part of the fun of being with you."

"I think," Killy said, "that I am trying to memorize everything I've seen—to have it all part of me forever."

"You will have much to write about when you get home." Fabrio gave her a quick glance. "What are you laughing at?"

"I was just thinking that if this were a summer vacation, I would finally have something to write about when the English teacher asked for a composition on how I spent my summer."

"Why? Have all your summers been boring?"

"I got so tired of trying to make them sound interesting that one year I manufactured an entire vacation. It was a car trip through the Canadian Rockies and into California. I got most of the information from a guidebook."

"What happened?" Fabrio was smiling.

"When I got an A on the composition, Mom and I agreed I should tell the teacher that it was a phony and accept the consequences. The teacher was very understanding, praised my imagination, and reduced the grade to a C."

They both laughed and Fabrio reached over and squeezed her hand. They were now on the open road going away from the city. Killy closed her eyes and breathed in the sweet smell as they rode through the pine woods. She wanted to remember that scent always.

When Killy heard the crunching of gravel under the wheels, she opened her eyes. Fabrio was easing the van between two open iron gates. "We're here? Fabrio, is this the villa? It's so impressive—more like a monastery than a house."

"It *was* built as a monastery, originally. And if it looks old, it is because it is about four centuries old. We can look around later. Right now we should wheel these racks into the room the models will be using. If you can unload them, I will go and check the arrangement of the chairs and see that the lighting is set for the runway."

Being part of the fashion world is fun for a day, but I wouldn't want a career of this, thought Killy, as she loaded the last of the dresses into the models' room. It was a beautiful room with deep red upholstery and old tapestries on the walls. *If this were my villa, I would make this my bedroom.*

"Killy! Can you come down here, please?" Fabrio was calling from the courtyard below.

She walked to the balcony and looked down. "I'm finished. Do you need me for something?"

"Yes. Come on down. The photographers want to test the lights. I think they would rather have you posing on the runway instead of me. Guess who you remind me of standing up there?"

"Who?"

"Juliet on the balcony." Fabrio was laughing.

"All right, Romeo, I'm on my way." Killy ran out of the room and down the marble spiral stairway.

How on earth can models stand this? Killy wondered as she stood alone on the runway. She felt awkward and very conspicuous until she saw Fabrio looking very proud of her.

"They aren't really taking pictures, are they?" Killy called to Fabrio.

"Do not talk. Walk." He laughed.

She walked all the way to the end of the runway. It seemed a mile long. At the end Fabrio picked her up and swung her to the floor. "You looked like a professional model up there. You are so beautiful today." He took her face in his hands and brushed her lips lightly with a kiss.

Later, when the villa was all but empty, they stood alone under the arcade of arches, looking out over the city. Killy looked sad. "I think I could stay in this very spot forever. It's going to be so hard to leave tomorrow."

"Do not look so unhappy. You know there is a part of you anxious to see your mother and your friends. You told me so the other day. And then there is the boy Tom you have mentioned. He must miss you terribly."

"Oh, Fabrio, I have a confession to make. I only mentioned Tom's name once or twice so you wouldn't think I was a total loser back in America. I really only dated him once, and he'll never ask me again. Something very embarrassing happened on our first date. And I'm such a baby, I just couldn't handle it. I understand completely why Tom wouldn't want to see me again. It's not his fault."

"But, Killy, what are you talking about? You are such a mature and confident person. That's one of the first things I noticed about you. What terrible thing happened on your date? And what did this boy Tom say to you to make you so sad?"

So Killy broke down and told Fabrio all about her disastrous date.

"You mean his friends laughed because you delivered newspapers?" At that point Fabrio laughed. "Killy, do you know how many jokes I have had to hear about driving around with dresses in my car? It is how you handle the jokes that is important. I learned that if you show you are hurt, the jokers win. Show confidence and the jokers lose."

To Killy, what he was saying made sense.

"What about your friend Tom? Did he laugh also?" Fabrio asked.

"No, he didn't laugh, but I can imagine how he must have felt."

"Now I am confused. Did you not discuss it with Tom?"

"I was afraid to hear how he felt about it. He tried to talk to me, but I brushed him off."

"Brushed? What?" Fabrio was often puzzled by her expressions.

"It means I wouldn't listen to him . . . changed the subject . . . walked away."

"Then you will never know until you ask him—talk to him about what happened. And when you ask him, if he is worth knowing, he will understand. Whatever way it ends, you will at least have an answer." Fabrio put his arm around her, and they stood looking at the distant city.

"I'm glad you brought me here today." Killy could make out the massive red dome of the cathedral. It looked like a toy from this distance. "You have given me so much, Fabrio. I will remember Florence and you always."

"I have much to thank you for, too. I had the chance to be a tourist in my own city, and you have helped me to love it more than I ever did. And you give me too much credit. You have taught me something. Remember I was ready to judge you by some of the other American girls I had seen? I will never do that again. That was childish."

Hand in hand, they walked back to the van. In such a short time, Killy thought, Fabrio had come to mean so much to her. He had been her teacher, her guide, and most of all, her friend. And because of him, she now had the confidence to face Tom. She turned to look back for one last view of the city, but they were too far away. She could barely make out the red dome of the cathedral.

Chapter Ten

It's all a myth—culture shock—jet lag. I won't succumb to it, Killy said to herself as she sat on the airplane that was taking her home. The last twelve hours had been hectic ones. Packing was only part of it—trying to squeeze the gifts she had bought into an already full suitcase. Andrea had made an elegant farewell dinner and set a beautiful table, despite her meager supply of plates, knives, and forks. And on Killy's plate she had placed a present of two tortoise-shell combs. Best of all was Andrea's insistence that Killy return again to visit.

On top of that, Jill had surprised Killy with a last-minute decision: Killy would be flying home alone. Jill was going to Paris for the weekend before returning to work.

Killy didn't mind going home alone. In fact, it made her feel more grown-up—a seasoned traveler. Besides, she thought Jill's going to Paris was an exciting idea—her aunt was as spontaneous as ever.

Killy had grown so much closer to her aunt in the last two weeks. Even though they hadn't spent much time together, they had shared some of their most private thoughts. Could Killy ever talk to her mother the way Jill had suggested she should? She was thinking about that, with the drone of the engines almost putting her to sleep, when she remembered the envelope.

Inside her purse was a large envelope she had found outside her door on the way to the airport. Fabrio must have put it there long after they had all gone to bed. Now she reached for it and tore it open.

Inside was a small, green, leather-bound book with blank pages. Fabrio had written on the first page, "This is for you to write your poems or stories in—or whatever you want. But promise to show them to me someday."

There was also another note attached to a photograph. Killy couldn't believe it. The photograph had been taken the day before at the villa. There she was in the lime green dress.

She read Fabrio's note. "I kept one of these

for myself. You cannot imagine the rush to get this developed and delivered to you before you left. When you look at this picture, I want you to remember how beautiful and special you are and how confident you can look."

Her eyes filled with tears. She looked down at the lime green dress she was wearing again today. Jill had given it to her as a present because she said it was meant for her coloring. Killy closed her eyes, and before her was the panorama of Florence as she had seen it from the villa. It was very real.

Sometime during that day, fatigue did hit her. It was probably while she was standing in line waiting to clear customs with at least fifty people ahead of her. Her legs throbbed, and her head ached—or vice versa. But once she was through and had her passport back, she felt a new surge of energy when saw her mother, Meg, and Carrie all waving at her.

At first they all said they didn't recognize her. Her mother was watching for someone in a blue shirtdress, and Meg proclaimed Killy's over-all appearance to be "different." It had to be the hairstyle, Carrie decided. "It's you, but it's not you," Carrie said as she hugged her friend.

"Carrie, you're perfectly clear as always." Killy laughed. It *was* good to see them all.

Later, back at home, Killy had to shake her cat Timmy awake to get so much as a yawn from him. She wandered through the downstairs rooms like a visitor in her own house. "It's all the same, but it seems different."

"That's what I said at the airport, and you all laughed at me," Carrie said, pouting, and they all laughed again.

The gifts she had bought were a success. Her mother's was a small leather evening bag, Carrie's was a long silk scarf in shades of blue and lavender, and Meg's was a porcelain perfume bottle with the Medici seal on the lid.

"Now tell us about the boy you wrote about in the postcard . . . David or something." Carrie was sitting cross-legged on the floor, looking up at Killy like a child waiting to hear a story.

"It was Fabrio, Carrie. David was the statue pictured on the front of the card."

Meg lost her usual composure and fell back on the sofa, laughing. Killy shook her head in disbelief, but she was glad to be home and with her friends again. Hearing the two of them again had Killy thinking she'd never been away. Still riding on the wave of excitement from her trip, she delivered an animated monologue on her adventures in Florence. The more she talked, the more her memories came alive. When she spoke of Fabrio, it was with a tenderness she had never used in describing another person.

"There were so many little things we did together. Once he picked me up at five-thirty in the morning to take me to see these famous bronze doors. He said it was the only time when I could see them without tourists around."

Killy was beginning to wind down. She was feeling tired, and looking at the clock, she realized she'd been talking for almost an hour.

Her mother stood up when Killy stopped talking. "Kids, I think Killy has had it for today. I think the hours she lost flying home today have finally caught up with her." Killy nodded in weary agreement.

Meg jumped up to leave, and Carrie agreed to join her only if Killy promised to tell "everything" the next day. Killy didn't really know what Carrie meant by that, but nodded anyway.

Upstairs, after the girls had left, Killy's room greeted her like an old friend. She realized she had missed the warm oak furniture and her window seat with the patchwork cushion. She was slowly unpacking clothes when her mother came into the room.

"Don't bother unpacking everything now.

We can do it tomorrow when you're not as tired. Sit on the bed with me for a while and talk to me. You know, I missed you, kiddo."

Killy let her mother hold her in her arms, and then she sat up. "I missed you too. Sometimes I wished you were there with me."

"Only sometimes?" her mother said teasingly.

"Well, especially when I'd see something and think to myself that you would like it. We've never really taken a trip together or seen a new place together."

"Does it bother you, honey, that we've never been able to afford to travel?" her mother asked gently.

"I guess right now it bothers me more that you've never had a chance to do anything and I've already been to Italy."

"You make me sound like a poor, suffering drudge." Her mother laughed.

"Well, don't you wish that you could have had a life like Aunt Jill's?"

"Then where would you be?"

"Seriously, Mom."

"I *am* being serious. I wouldn't trade being your mother for the world—or a world cruise *or* a fast-paced job. But I will tell you that I'm working on getting a better job. With all the excitement of your coming home today, I was going to wait until tomorrow to tell you about it."

"No, tell me now. I'm really not so tired that I can't listen. And you seem excited about it. I can see it in your face."

"My company has started a management training program, and I'm being considered for it." She took a deep breath and continued. "They'd pay my tuition. I'd have to go to school three nights a week and all day Friday, but with the credits I already have, I could have my degree by the time *you* graduate next year. And, Killy, the job would give us both more. We could even take a *real* trip through the Rockies!"

"Mom, that's super. I can't believe all this happened while I was away."

"Remember, I don't have the appointment yet, so don't get your hopes up, and neither will I."

"Now you sound just like a mother! Of course you'll get it, and we'll have the biggest celebration ever!"

"Well, let's just wait and see, OK?"

"It sure is good to be home," Killy said and yawned.

"It sure is good to have you back, honey. You've changed since you've been away. I don't know what it is exactly—what Carrie called 'different.' I guess I'd call it more grown-up. Get ready for bed now, and I'll see you in the morning." She kissed Killy good night.

The bed felt so good, and the sheets smelled like home. It had been such a long day. Killy closed her eyes, and dreamed of lavender blue hills just like the ones outside of Florence.

Chapter Eleven

It was a spring rite at Ridgefield High. The Junior Class Carnival—the last day of spring break, an upbeat ending to the last vacation of the school year. Killy would have forgotten it entirely if Carrie hadn't called to remind her. Two weeks earlier, Killy thought, she probably wouldn't have wanted to go. It was as though her trip to Italy had been a turning point for her. She felt better about herself, eager to find out if she could fit in with the rest of her class. Killy believed this sudden spurt of self-confidence was mainly Fabrio's doing.

As she brushed her hair into its new style, she looked at the picture of herself in the lime green dress. "Confident Killy," she repeated to herself, afraid of losing her courage. In less than half an hour, she was supposed to meet Meg and Carrie and head for the carnival. Killy realized that she would probably be seeing Tom that afternoon. How this "new" Killy would handle meeting him, she didn't know. But in the back of her mind, she remembered what Fabrio had said about how people worth knowing will be understanding. She was determined not to brood or worry about what she would say to Tom. She would just wait until she saw him, and then say what she was feeling.

Junior Carnival was held not only to cure the back-to-school doldrums but also to raise money for a class trip in June. There was a small admission charge, and books of tickets were sold for a variety of skill games, including one that allowed kids to pitch a ball and try to hit a bar that would dunk one of their teachers into a tank of water.

The three girls arrived at the carnival in high spirits. With all the activity and the rush of kids, it seemed unlikely that Killy would spot Tom right away. But she did, and Kim was very much with him, tugging playfully at his shirt-sleeve. Carrie had run off to try to "sock it to" her algebra teacher at the dunking booth. Meg and Killy had joined a group of kids from the newspaper and yearbook staffs who were seated around picnic tables at the far end of the gym.

From a safe distance, Killy watched Tom at the weight-lifting booth, with Kim bouncing alongside him, urging him on. One of the kids at the table was asking Killy about her trip, but she was staring at Tom so hard that she didn't hear the question at first.

"The trip? Oh! The trip. I'm sorry, I was thinking of something else. It was wonderful. It was like living a book—a novel about a girl who has never been anywhere and is suddenly in a romantic, faraway city, living a life she has always dreamed about."

Killy stopped abruptly and glanced at the group to see if anyone was laughing at her. No one was. In fact, everyone seemed to be waiting to hear more. When had she ever had the attention of so many kids before? She smiled to herself and continued with stories about Florence, making the kids laugh when she imitated the policeman directing traffic.

"Did your nanny go with you to Italy?" Killy didn't have to turn around to know that Kim had approached the group.

"Why, *of course* nanny couldn't go. She had to stay home in my nursery and take care of my teddy and duckie and all my dolls," Killy said in a little girl's voice.

Everyone roared. Killy continued with her story about the bronze door caper, and from the corner of her eye, she could see Kim shrugging her shoulders and walking away.

When the group broke up to go back to the games, Tom came over to her. He seemed even more handsome than he had been two weeks ago. In the seconds that passed before she spoke, she knew she still cared for him.

"I'd like to talk to you soon, OK?" he asked. She couldn't tell from his tone of voice whether he was angry at her or not. Fighting back the assumption that he was, she smiled at him.

"Yes, I'd like that," she said. Just then a clown ran up to tickle her nose with a giant daisy. Killy laughed, and Tom smiled at the way she wrinkled her nose. *He's not angry,* she said to herself, and suddenly she felt at ease.

"I guess this isn't really the place to talk," she said.

"No, I guess not."

"Did you win at weight lifting?" She had an idea he hadn't.

"No. Did you know you could get hurt doing that? I'll stick with basketball."

"You can get hurt doing that, too. Remember?"

He looked at her carefully for a minute, and then his face softened to a gentle smile. "Yeah, I remember." And then she heard Kim calling him, breaking up their quiet moment.

"Listen," he said, "I promised to act as judge for the arm wrestling. You're right. It's too crazy here for us to really talk. But I want you to promise that tomorrow we will. Promise me that, Killy."

"I promise," she said softly.

"The only thing I want to tell you now is that you look beautiful, Killy. You really do. See you tomorrow, OK?"

"OK. Bye." She was so stunned that she didn't even respond to his compliment, but his words echoed in her mind long after he had gone. *But what about Kim? How did she fit into the picture?* Killy wondered.

"Going back to school tomorrow certainly hasn't put you in a post-vacation depression," her mother said that night. "You look like you had a terrific time today. I still remember how much fun the junior carnival used to be when I was in high school."

"You mean they had them all the way back then?" Killy liked teasing her mother about the "olden days" at Ridgefield.

"They sure did, but that's all ancient history, right? Why don't you bring me up to date? You can start by explaining those stars in your eyes."

"It was a great day, Mom. For the first time since I've been in that class, I really feel a part of it. I think I owe it all to Fabrio."

"Why Fabrio?"

"He taught me to think more of myself, to be confident."

"But it took *you* to make it happen. Don't forget that." She tried to make her next question sound casual. "Did you see Tom today?"

Killy tried to sound equally casual. She wasn't sure she was ready to discuss Tom with her mother yet. "Yeah, I did. Why?"

"Oh, then he must have told you," her mother said, smiling.

"Told me what? Mom, what are you talking about?" Killy caught her mother's expression. It was one of those "now I've done it" looks.

"I'm sorry. I just assumed that if you saw him he must have told you. He didn't want me to mention it, but as long as I've gone this far, I guess I have to tell you. Remember the boy, Josh, you got to deliver your papers while you were away?" Killy nodded but was still puzzled. "He broke his leg the day after you left, and I couldn't find anyone else to take the route. So I started doing it myself before work."

"Mom, that makes me feel awful. You have enough to do."

"That's not the end of the story. You see, Tom saw me one morning and offered to do the route until you got back. He just asked me not to tell you. But I assumed he just wanted to tell you himself."

"I don't believe this. Tom did that for *me*?"

"He wouldn't even take any money for it. He's quite a guy, Killy. And I think he's crazy about you."

"Well, I don't know about that, Mom."

"Just wait and see. I can tell I'm right. Now I'm going upstairs to take a long bath. If you don't mind, why don't you use some of your new Italian cooking expertise and start setting up the lasagna for tomorrow night's dinner. And don't burn the pot!"

Killy went to the kitchen and started heating a pot of water for the lasagna noodles. She sat at the kitchen table, thinking. Her mother was so sure that things were going to work out with Tom. Killy really wanted to believe that. But what about Kim? How could Tom really be interested in her—Killy—with someone like Kim around all the time?

Chapter Twelve

Something was living in Killy's locker. It was green and protruded through the three air slots at the top of the locker door. Killy looked at it in amazement. Someone else noticed the leafy-green growth and stopped to stare at it too. Before long there was a small crowd waiting for her to open the locker. Killy hesitated, then slowly reached for the handle and flung open the door. Everyone jumped back a step.

"My plants! They've been in here for two weeks. They should be dead by now, but they're still growing!" Everyone laughed and congratulated Killy for having a "green thumb." She laughed too. Then the bell rang, and everyone headed for his or her homeroom. But as she reached into her locker to find her books, she heard a voice behind her.

"Didn't someone do a science fiction movie about plants like those?"

She knew who it was before she even turned around. "Hi, Tom. If I don't get them out of here soon, they may take over the whole school."

"Let's talk today . . . after school, OK?" He took her smile to mean yes. "I'll pick you up out front right after the last period."

When Killy thought about him during the day, she could feel her cheeks burning. She wondered if anyone else noticed. Meg did, during gym.

"You look flushed, and we haven't even started to run yet."

"Maybe I'm just anticipating how I'll feel after two laps around the field," Killy said jokingly.

"Killy, you can't fool me," Meg said as the two of them began to run side by side. "Something's going on between you and Tom. I know it."

"Meg, what I want to know is what's going on between Tom and Kim. Are they seeing each other?"

"Seeing or dating?"

"Whatever," Killy responded.

"There's a difference. I was *seeing* Andy this year. Jenny and Scott are *dating.* Kim and Jack date on and off—one of those love/hate relationships. I think she was *seeing* Tom during the vacation break." Meg sounded like an English teacher giving a grammar lesson.

"I think I'm sorry I asked," Killy said, laughing. "I guess I'll have to ask him myself. I'm meeting him after school today. He wants to talk about that terrible date we had."

"You still don't want to talk about that, do you? It's OK. I understand. But I think Carrie was hurt. You know, you ought to trust your friends more, Killy. Who knows? We may even be able to help from time to time." Meg smiled as she spoke the last words.

"I'll remember that, Meg, I promise. And thanks for saying that. If you don't mind, I'm going to run ahead, now, OK? I think I have a lot of energy to burn off."

"Go ahead. I'm going to go over my lines for Saint Joan and try to get more into the character."

Killy ran ahead until she was all by herself. She spent the rest of the period daydreaming about Tom.

*　　*　　*

"First of all, I'm not going to apologize," Tom said as he pulled out of the school parking lot.

"For what?" She looked at him.

"For calling you a baby that day. You acted like one."

"Thank you," she said quietly.

"For what?" Now his eyes left the road for a second to look at her.

"For doing my newspapers." They shot a quick look at each other and laughed.

"Now we sound like Cary Grant and Katharine Hepburn in *Pat and Mike*."

"That was Spencer Tracy, not Cary Grant." Killy could barely get the words out because she was laughing so hard.

"Here we go again!" he said.

"What movie is *that* from?"

"It's not from any movie. I was just thinking of the first time you came into the hospital room." He paused. "Welcome back."

"Thank you. It's good to be back."

"Shh! If you say one more word, I won't be able to keep this car on the road." They had a silent understanding for the rest of the ride. They didn't say a word, but looked at each other from time to time and smiled.

Tom drove into the country. He wanted to

show Killy the stables where he had worked before moving to Ridgefield. He parked behind a barn next to a corral and was immediately recognized by an old friend. A sad-eyed chestnut mare bobbed her head up and down to greet him.

"Come on, Killy, meet Sissy."

"She's beautiful. Why is she called Sissy?"

"She shies and gets skittish a lot, but I know why. She just wants to be talked to and handled gently. I used to know her so well that I felt as if I owned her. Let's walk over past the paddock into the field."

"No wonder you liked your job here. It's so peaceful and so far away from everything. Tom, do you mind if I tell you something I've been dying to say?"

"No, Killy. I have some things I want to say to you."

"I'm sorry I never gave you a chance to explain about that night at the Hero Factory. And before that, I'm sorry I never told you how old I was or that I didn't want you telling anyone about my newspaper route. I don't even care anymore who knows about the newspapers. At least I'm earning money for the things I want, not having them handed to me. It wasn't until this spring break that I realized that I should be proud of handling two jobs and school."

"Look, I don't need to know a girl's birth date before I ask her out. I asked you out that time because I liked you and wanted to know you better. If you've decided to be proud of your jobs, then you should also be proud of how much you've accomplished for your age. Besides, it's how you act that counts. And you act and *look* like a junior."

"You sound like someone I met on vacation."

"Sunday, when I saw you at the carnival, you looked so pretty, and I wanted to hear what you were saying that made everyone laugh. But I was afraid you were going to give me the brush-off the way you did that Monday after our date. Now I can see that you've changed." Tom stopped and looked into her eyes. "Killy, I want us to go back to the way we were at the hospital. I want us to really get to know each other. I want to take you out and let the world know you're my girl." Tom had taken both her hands in his.

"But what about Kim? I thought you and she were—"

"Friends. Kim is OK once you get to know her. We helped each other through a boring vacation, but that's all. I know she still cares for Jack. She's the first to admit that she wanted to make him jealous. I think things will work out for them as soon as Kim learns to be herself and stops acting like a spoiled baby. I told her so."

"You did?" Killy was smiling, but she felt so emotional that there was also a tear running down her cheek.

"You're the only girl I want, Killy." Tom embraced her tenderly. Then he smiled. "Let me take you to see *Pat and Mike* and prove I'm right about Cary Grant." He pressed her head to his chest, softly caressing her hair.

It all felt like a dream, but she knew it was real.

"You're wrong," she said, smiling up at him, looking into his eyes. "But I'll go anyway."

He tilted her head back and kissed her lightly. "We'll see," he whispered.

Chapter Thirteen

She was right about Spencer Tracy, but she didn't gloat. Tom took the defeat good-naturedly and squeezed her hand when the film credits rolled onto the screen.

Since their "reunion"—as they called it—at the stables, they had been dating steadily. Together, they had seen Meg give an outstanding performance as Joan of Arc. But their relationship was not restricted to official dates. Sometimes they just did homework together or went for walks, savoring their first spring together.

Sometimes Tom picked her up at the hospital after work. Killy liked having him come back with her to the house. She liked watching him watching her while she fixed her tea or poured a soda for him. There was something reassuring about having him in her own familiar surroundings—watching him play with the cat, having him help with the dishes when her mother invited him to dinner.

One afternoon when he met her at the hospital, she came bursting through the lobby door, jumped up, and put her arms around his neck. Her boss had just asked her to work more hours each week at the gift shop. That meant she could finally give up the newspaper route. They celebrated when they got to her house by stacking wood in the fireplace and ceremoniously lighting it with that morning's newspaper. They didn't seem to care that the weather was much too warm for a fire.

If Killy had to work late in the newsroom after school, Tom would work out in the gym waiting for her. One May afternoon he popped into the newsroom before heading for the gym. Killy was talking to herself and throwing balls of paper at the wastebasket.

"Not a bad dunk shot." Tom stood in the doorway, smiling. "What's wrong? This morning, on the way to school, you were so happy that you were throwing dandelion blossoms in the air and saying something about chasing

126

away the demons of winter." Since no one else was around, he kissed her quickly.

"Don't tease. I don't think I'm up to it. Look at this." She handed him a memo from Mrs. Gillen.

He read it, then said, "Great. A dance is a good way to raise money for the newspaper, and Mrs. Gillen must think you can handle being chairperson, or she wouldn't have appointed you."

"But did you see the name of the person I'm supposed to work with? Kim! Tom, I can't speak to her, let alone work with her and expect her to take orders from me. You know, this is the first time I've been asked to do anything like this, and I *want* to do it. But right now I feel like resigning and letting someone else take over."

"Calm down. You'll be on top of the situation in no time. Just remember—it's for a good cause. Do I have to give you another pep talk?" he asked, grinning.

"No. I can handle this—I think."

Suddenly Kim was right there in the same room with them, coming through the door and slamming it dramatically behind her.

"Am I interrupting? I could come back." It was the same tone of voice she used when she made fun of Killy.

"Oh, no, I'm on my way out, Kim," Tom said. "See you later, Killy." He gave a wink that only Killy could see and left.

Kim got right to the point. "Look, when I volunteered to work on this, I didn't know *you* were the chairman."

"Well, I didn't know *you* were going to be on the committee."

"And I didn't know *you* knew anything about dances. In fact, I didn't even know you were allowed out that late at night." Kim studied her long fingernails, refusing to look at Killy.

"That's it!" Killy stood up and walked to the window. "Let's cut it, Kim. Why don't you just tell me what it is you have against me? Why can't you ever leave me alone?"

Kim was stunned and mumbled something Killy couldn't quite hear.

"I didn't hear you, Kim."

"If you must know, I'm jealous."

"Jealous? All these years? Of what?" Killy couldn't believe her ears.

"You wouldn't understand."

"Try me." Killy looked hard at Kim's large green eyes.

"Everything is easy for you. You get A's without even trying, it seems. I give up a date to cram for a test, stay up all night studying, and still barely pull a C. It's just not fair."

Killy started to laugh. "And it's not funny either," Kim said, pouting.

"Do you know what you sound like?" Killy was still laughing.

They looked at one another and said the word simultaneously. "A baby." Then Kim grinned and both of them burst into laughter.

"You know what, Kim? I've always been jealous of you."

"Me? Why?"

"Oh, for little things like your hair always staying in place, your rainbow of silk blouses, your fingernails that never get broken in gym class, the way you have with boys. Shall I go on?"

"My fingernails!" Kim was laughing hysterically, and her laughter was contagious.

By the time Tom came back, they had worked out the details of what they should do for the dance and were laughing again about the fingernails.

"I could hear you two all the way down the hall. What's going on?" Tom was clearly bewildered. The two girls looked at his expression and started giggling again.

*   *   *

She and Tom walked Kim home. Tom tried to listen as both girls explained their ideas for the fund raiser at the same time.

"It's going to be more than a dance. Kim came up with a super suggestion. Tell him, Kim."

"Trash," Kim said, trying to keep a straight face.

"What?"

"Trash, as in garbage," Killy replied, without so much as a snicker.

"You're going to decorate the gym in trash. Well, I can see Mrs. Gillen is going to be so happy she picked you two." Tom shook his head, still confused.

"No," Kim said, "but I better explain this before you think we've both lost our minds. It's not going to be a dance—that wouldn't get enough money. Instead, it's going to be a double fund raiser. We're going to clean up the town!"

"You're going to rob stores in town? Count me out!"

"No, silly. Kim's idea is to get a group of kids to volunteer to pick up trash in town the day before the dance. For every bag they fill, we get store owners and other people in town to pledge money. It means cleaning down by the brook, in the park, and all over downtown. It's the kind of campaign that will interest the local newspapers. And the reward for all the volunteers will be the dance!"

Now Tom was sharing the girls' excitement. He put an arm around each of them and gave them a hug.

"You two are some team. Is it OK to say that it comes as quite a surprise? Actually, *shock* might be a better word."

Tom and Killy left a smiling Kim at her door and walked on toward Killy's. She felt more than pleased with the way things had turned out with Kim. She was delighted.

"You're wonderful," Tom said.

"So are you," she said softly, holding his hand.

"No, I mean whatever happened with you and Kim today, I think you did it. And I'm proud of you."

"Don't give me all the credit. Kim had a lot to do with it, too. Someday I'll tell you about it." She raised his hand and twirled under his arm. Tom caught her by the waist. Killy felt as though she had known him forever. He was so much a part of her thoughts and her happy frame of mind. No, she couldn't imagine life without Tom.

Chapter Fourteen

The green, leather book Fabrio had given her was opened to a blank page. Killy began to write.

> *Spinning.*
> *Whirling.*
> *Sheathed in excitement.*
> *Dancing headlong into a wind.*

She put the pen down and looked out the window of her bedroom at the flowering apple tree. Killy checked to see if there was any activity in the birdhouse Tom had hung for her the week before, and remembered his teasing her. "No bird wants to live in an apple tree. Just think of all that banging and knocking on the roof when the rotten apples start falling off."

Killy turned back to the poem and jumped when the door flew open, breaking her solitude. "I'm sorry, honey, but I raced home to tell you. Almost had a speeding ticket but talked my way out of it. Killy," her mother said catching her breath, "I got it. The appointment to the management program—I did it."

"Oh, Mom, I *knew* you would. I'm so happy for you." The two of them hugged and did several steps of what faintly resembled a tap dance. "Great, Mom. An executive who can dance. Add that to your resumé. How do we celebrate?"

"Any way that doesn't require cooking. What about going to that new gourmet takeout place and buying a smorgasbord of things? We could invite Tom to come if you like. I know you usually see him on Friday nights . . . and Saturday and Sunday and—"

"Why don't *we* go? Just the two of us! I didn't have anything definite with Tom tonight." Killy went back to her desk and closed the green book.

"Anything wrong between you and Tom? You seemed a little pensive when I walked in—sorry, barged in—here."

"No, everything is fine with Tom. Maybe it's even too fine." Killy looked thoughtful.

"What do you mean?"

"When you came in, I was writing a poem in the book Fabrio gave me. It seems as though I should have been able to fill this book by now, but I don't seem to have time to write anymore." Killy went to the window and flopped on the window seat. "Oh, Mom, sometimes I think things are going too fast with Tom and me. I love being with him, and we have so much fun, but I don't want us to become too serious, and I don't want to spend *all* my time with him."

It was the first time she had talked seriously about her relationship with Tom, and her mother let her continue. "I like being independent, too. I didn't realize how much until I went to Italy. For the first time in my life, I was really doing things on my own, spending time in a museum all by myself, even flying home alone. I don't want to lose Tom, but I don't want to end up headed for—" Killy stopped short.

"Marriage?" Her mother finished the thought.

"I'm sorry. I wasn't thinking. I didn't mean to hurt you by saying that. It's just that I have my whole life ahead of me. I guess I'm scared to get too serious now."

"You haven't hurt me, honey. You're not me. You're your own person—with your own dreams and your own needs. I know what a confusing time this is for you. But you know what?" Killy turned to look at her mother. Her eyes were misty. "You're stronger now than you've ever been. Tell Tom how you feel. Tell him you're scared, if you want. I think he'll understand. I think you're wise to be cautious and careful and to think about your future. Just promise me you'll give yourself—and Tom—a chance."

"I promise, Mom. Thanks for listening."

"It's part of my job—a new part, but I like it the best." She held Killy close and kissed her cheek. "Now, why don't we go and get our celebration dinner?"

In a moment Killy had perked up. She held the door open for her mother. "I have a craving for something exotic like stuffed grape leaves," she said.

She had just picked up the Saturday mail when the phone rang. She knew it would be Tom.

"Missed you last night. Did you have a good time celebrating with your mom?"

"Don't you ever say hello? Yes, we had fun swapping and sampling food. I think Mom's hooked on Oriental salad, and I was as stuffed as a grape leaf." She laughed at her own joke.

"Can I pick you up after work?"

"Uh-huh."

"See ya, sweetheart."

"Your Bogart impersonation is still bad. See you later."

That night she and Tom would be going to the Hero Factory again. It was Tom's idea. He said he wanted to show her how their first date *should* have gone. She thought it was a very romantic idea and wanted very much to go—to dance with him for the first time.

She left the mail on the hall table and settled herself in the blue velvet chair near the fireplace. There were no flickering flames to gaze at, but her thoughts did drift back to the afternoon they had made the celebration fire together. *I have to talk to him*, she thought. *But not tonight.*

He greeted her at the hospital, a sly grin on his face, and handed her a small, gift-wrapped box.

"It's not my birthday."

"I know. Open it."

Inside was a statue of a turtle, standing upright, wearing a pained look, and holding a bowling ball.

Killy laughed. "I love him! But why—?"

"To remind you of the first part of our first date."

"Oh, Tom. Did I ever tell you how wonderful you are?"

He didn't have to answer her question. His warm embrace said it all.

It was still daylight when they reached the Hero Factory, and the old building didn't look nearly as ominous as it had that cold March night. Inside it seemed more subdued. The lighting didn't seem as harsh or the music as loud as they had the night of their first date. Maybe she was just more relaxed and ready to enjoy the atmosphere, Killy thought.

"Over here, Tom." History was repeating itself. Kim was calling them to join her group. Killy stiffened slightly, and Tom noticed it right away. "Remember, everything is different now," he said as he took her hand to lead her to the table.

"You're right. For an instant there I thought I was living in the past. Let's go join them," she said, giving his hand a squeeze.

Kim winked at Killy as she sat down. "Hi, Killy . . . Tom. I'm glad you're here, Killy, I'm trying to get some more recruits for our clean-up drive. Scott here says he doesn't take out the trash at home, so why should he haul some-body else's?"

"I don't do windows, either." Scott ducked as Kim took a swipe at him.

Everyone laughed. "Scott," Killy said slyly, "do you like seeing your name in our newspaper and reading the recap of your football games?"

Scott knew what she was getting at. "Yes, sure. My mom and dad cherish every word." He laughed.

"Well then, if you'd like to have a school newspaper in September, you'd better come haul with the rest of us."

"And that goes for all of you," Kim added. And then she whispered to Killy, "I think you did it. I think you shamed them into coming and helping." Killy beamed with pride.

"Could we move away from garbage and get into the menu? I'm starving," Tom said, hand-ing her a menu. She took it and wondered why everyone was looking at her—almost waiting for a reaction.

Then she knew. Under "Sports Star Spe-cials" the menu read, "#7, Tom Thompson."

"They name *sandwiches* after you guys?" Killy burst into laughter, and everyone smiled at her surprise.

Jack leaned toward Killy. "Only until we

graduate. Then the sandwiches don't change, but the names do."

"Well, I'm definitely ordering a number seven," Killy said, then laughed.

"I don't know if it's an honor or not," Tom said with some dismay. "Mine includes turkey."

"You think that's bad," said Kim. "I can't even order a 'Jack Compton' special. It's chopped liver!" With that remark, their table became the noisiest one in the place.

When the soft rock music started, Jack led Kim from the table. The others followed, including Tom and Killy.

"For a couple who never danced together before, we're not bad." Tom smiled down at her. She rested her cheek on his chest, keeping time more to his slow, rhythmic breathing than the music.

"We're just like Fred Astaire and Ginger Rogers," he whispered into her ear.

"Don't you dare break this mood by making me laugh!" Killy looked up at him, and their faces almost touched. They danced in silence after that, oblivious to everyone and everything except each other.

Chapter Fifteen

BAG FOR BUCKS! Killy held the poster as Carrie drove the thumbtack into the cork board.

"That's the last one," Killy said. "We'll just stick the sign-up sheet next to it. I didn't realize how much work was involved in a project like this. Thanks for letting me count on you."

"Any time," Carrie said. She made a sweeping bow.

"Hey, wasn't it fun the other night at the Hero Factory? I was so surprised when you walked in with Bill and Meg showed up with Andy. That was the first time we triple-dated. But why didn't you tell me you were going?"

"You don't tell *us* everything, do you?" Carrie's mood had changed, and Killy remembered what Meg had said about Carrie being hurt before.

"I'm sorry, Carrie. I never meant to hide anything from you two. But when I first met Tom and had that date with him last March, I didn't know what to say to anyone. I didn't know what I was feeling. There was so much spinning around inside me."

"That's what friends are for, Killy—to help you figure things out," Carrie insisted.

"I think I'm starting to understand that now. I've always felt close to you two, but I've just never been able to really open up to other people. I want to change all that."

"Then you'll start confiding in us?" Carrie asked.

"I'll work on it." Killy smiled. "You know, habits don't change overnight. Bear with me, OK?"

"Sure. What are friends for?" Carrie said, dramatically placing her hand on her chest.

Giggling with her friend in the hallway, Killy felt as though she were back in the third grade again. *Only then*, she thought, as they started down the corridor, *the biggest decision I had to make was what game to play after school.*

"Where's Meg?" Killy asked.

"You sent her to canvass store owners for pledges, remember?"

"Oh, I forgot. I sent Tom, too, and I'm supposed to meet him later. Do you want to come along?"

"Killy, you've got me getting pledges from my neighbors today! Our forgetful leader!"

They were out in the bright sunlight, and Carrie was putting on her red, plastic sunglasses. "Carrie, I'm going to head into town and find Tom. Call me later and let me know how you did with the pledges."

It isn't like me, Killy said to herself, *to forget details like that. And I know what's distracting me! One wonderful evening with Tom, and I push aside what I was determined to do. I'm going to talk to him today. I've got to let him know what's worrying me before I'm so deeply involved that I can't think straight.*

Downtown, Killy began looking in store windows, hoping to spot Tom. She knew she was early for their arranged meeting at the corner of Summit and Commerce, but she thought she might still run into him. No luck in the tailor's shop or the shoe store. Farther on down the street, she caught sight of him. He was backing out of the beauty salon, blushing. She had never seen him so flustered. She had to laugh.

"Tom!" He looked around, relieved to see her.

"What happened? You look funny."

"From now on *you* do the beauty shops. Killy, you wouldn't believe it! The things women were having done to their heads. One woman was wrapped in tinfoil, and another was sitting under an orange lamp that made her face look like a Halloween mask. But then, as I was leaving, the worst happened."

"What?" Killy asked.

"There was a woman with electrodes sticking out of her head and attached to a computer of some sort. I thought she was having a brain transplant or something, and I guess I screamed when I backed into her."

"Oh, Tom! You should see your face. A brain transplant? That was the new precision hair dyeing. A timer goes off when the correct color is reached."

"I'm glad you showed up when you did. In fact, anytime you show up I'm glad," he said and took her hand.

She had been laughing, but she stopped suddenly. *It's not going to work*, she thought.

144

But she fought her impulse to run away and not face up to the conflict. "We have to talk, Tom."

"Killy, you're trembling. Let me hold you."

"No, don't hold me. It will only confuse me. Please, can we go somewhere and talk?"

"Do you want to cross over to the park?" She nodded without looking at him. "Killy, I'm worried about you. What's wrong?"

They waited for a break in the traffic, then crossed to the park entrance, near the playground.

"Do you want to sit over there?" Tom said, indicating a bench near the playground area.

"No, let's just walk."

"Tell me what's wrong." He now looked as nervous as she did.

"Tom, I don't know how to begin, so I guess I'm going to have to blurt this out in whatever way I can. I can't think of being away from you . . . and I can't think of being with you forever. This is getting serious, and I'm scared." She was twisting her hands as she spoke. When she was finished, Tom covered both her hands with his.

"Are you ready to listen? First, let me tell you that I've never known anyone quite like you, and I can't remember when I've felt this happy. But, Killy, I'm not thinking 'forever.' What I'm trying to do is take things as they come. There's still so much ahead for both of us—as individuals. I just want to know that I can share right now with you."

She was trying to absorb his words. "Killy, do you know the only plans I've thought of for us? I want to take you to the junior prom. I want to take you to the beach the first day of summer and dunk you. I even want to collect trash with you next week. That's not forever . . . it's now."

A tear was sliding down Killy's cheek. For one brief moment she remembered hearing words like that before from Fabrio, when they had stood facing the river in Florence. Then she looked up at Tom.

"Oh, Tom, that's what I want, too." They held each other, and she could feel his sigh of relief. "I want to walk in the park together just like we're doing now and have you at the newspaper dance beside me and let you dunk me and pick up trash—"

"Hey, your button is stuck on fast forward. You'll have us graduating any minute now."

"Senior year! I forgot about that and the class trip and—"

"And then we'll wait and see," he said, and put his finger to her lips to quiet her. Then he took it away and gently kissed her. When they parted, she whispered softly, "Yes, we'll wait and see."

Read these great new *Sweet Dreams* romances, on sale soon:

( ) **#29 NEVER LOVE A COWBOY by Jesse DuKore (On sale December 15, 1982 • 23101-4 • $1.95)**
Bitsy is thrilled when she moves from crowded New York City to colorful Austin, Texas, and even more thrilled when she sees handsome Billy Joe riding his horse to school. But even when Bitsy's new school radio program grabs everyone else's attention, Billy Joe's eye remains on gorgeous Betty Lou. Can a city girl like Bitsy ever win the heart of a Texas cowboy like Billy Joe?

( ) **#30 LITTLE WHITE LIES by Lois T. Fisher (On sale December 15, 1982 • 23102-2 • $1.95)**
Everyone says Nina has a good imagination—a gift for telling stories. In fact, it's one of her stories that attracts Scott to her. He's one of the Daltonites, the most sophisticated clique in the school. The Daltonites don't welcome outsiders, but Nina finds it so easy to impress them with a little exaggeration here, a white lie there. But her lies finally start to catch up with her, and Nina's afraid of losing Scott forever.

( ) **#31 TOO CLOSE FOR COMFORT by Debra Spector (On sale January 15, 1983 • 23189-8 • $1.95)**
For years Drea and Derek have been best friends. They've always loved each other, but when Derek asks Drea for a date, their feelings grow stronger, until finally they're *in love*. Then things start going sour for Drea. Is it because

Derek's becoming so possessive? Or because Sam Henessy's getting interested in her? Should Drea break up with Derek? And if they do, can they ever be friends again?

( ) #32 DAYDREAMER by Janet Quin-Harkin (On sale January 15, 1983 • 23190-1 • $1.95)
All too often, Lisa finds herself escaping into daydreams—dreams of fame, friends and boyfriends galore, Hollywood, her parents, and falling in love. But when her fantasy bubble bursts, she has to open her eyes to the fact that, in real life, things don't always work out the way they do in dreams.

( ) THE LOVE BOOK by Deidre Laiken & Alan Schneider (On sale January 15, 1983 • 23288-6 • $1.95)
If people could recognize true love at first glance, life (and love) would be a lot less complicated. But love is not always what it appears to be. The more you know about love, the more successful you'll be at finding and keeping it—and understanding love is what this, the first nonfiction *Sweet Dreams* book, is all about.

Buy these books at your local bookstore or use this handy coupon for ordering:

You'll fall in love with all the Sweet Dream romances.
Reading these stories, you'll be reminded of yourself or of
someone you know. There's Jennie, the *California Girl*,
who becomes an outsider when her family moves to Texas.
And Cindy, the *Little Sister*, who's afraid that Christine,
the oldest in the family, will steal her new boyfriend.
Don't miss any of the Sweet Dreams romances.

☐	22542	**LOVE SONG #19** **Anne park**	$1.95
☐	22682	**THE POPULARITY SUMMER #20** **Rosemary Vernon**	$1.95
☐	22607	**ALL'S FAIR IN LOVE #21** **Jeanne Andrews**	$1.95
☐	22683	**SECRET IDENTITY #22** **Joanna Campbell**	$1.95
☐	22840	**FALLING IN LOVE AGAIN #23** **Barbara Conklin**	$1.95
☐	22957	**THE TROUBLE WITH CHARLIE #24** **Jaye Ellen**	$1.95
☐	22543	**HER SECRET SELF #25** **Rhondi Villot**	$1.95
☐	22692	**IT MUST BE MAGIC #26** **Marian Woodruff**	$1.95
☐	22681	**TOO YOUNG FOR LOVE #27** **Gailanne Maravel**	$1.95
☐	23053	**TRUSTING HEARTS #28** **Jocelyn Saal**	$1.95